MW00414747

HELLMOUTH & HOT FLASHES

MYSTICAL MIDLIFE IN MAINE BOOK 3

BRENDA TRIM

Copyright © October 2021 by Brenda Trim
Editor: Chris Cain
Cover Art by Fiona Jayde

* * *

This book is a work of fiction. The names, characters, places, and incidents are products of the writers' imagination or have been used fictitiously and are not to be construed as real. Any resemblance to persons, living or dead, actual events, locales or organizations is entirely coincidental.

WARNING: The unauthorized reproduction of this work is illegal. Criminal copyright infringement is investigated by the FBI and is punishable by up to 5 years in federal prison and a fine of $250,000.

All rights reserved. With the exception of quotes used in reviews, this book may not be reproduced or used in whole or in part by any means existing without written permission from the authors.

❀ Created with Vellum

There is nothing more profound than creating something out of nothing.

CHAPTER 1

"*C*rap!" The knife slipped, and I almost cut the fingers off on my left hand. I hadn't been paying attention. Life had been pretty calm since I killed Myrna a couple months ago. Jean-Marc came for a visit, so I was grateful nothing magical ruined the time.

I knew I needed to tell him, but having him adjust to our new house and the business I'd inherited took a greater priority. Given the tension during Jean-Marc's visit, I was glad I hadn't tried to spring that on him, too. *Next time he'll be ready to hear about it.*

My mom's head turned in my direction. "What happened?"

I pulled the knife from the pumpkin I was carving. "I almost sliced my thumb off. I'm no good at this."

My mom and Nana had sold their house and moved into Nimaha with me, saying they didn't want to miss anything and I had plenty of room. I was happier than I expected to be about the prospect. Not having an official job outside the house like I was used to, I had spent significant time with the group over the past six months and couldn't imagine life without them here.

Nina laughed. "That's because dad always took the lead when we carved, saying as a surgeon he was better suited. You need to stop living by his rules and expectations, mom. You're better than he led you to believe."

"Oh, I know I am. It took me time to realize how much control he still had over me. I'm too preoccupied with the meeting with Lilith. She needs me to look over some contracts and decide on budget cuts."

I'd also been working closely with Lilith on the business. Silva Enterprises had more than half a dozen different companies. Each had a coven member at the helm. I was happy to give Lilith a raise and have her play a more prominent role so I could spend my time on the magical side of my life.

"You will find a balance between your business and your magic. Believe it or not, you still have a lot to learn. There will come a time when you will react instinctively and not need to chant when you cast."

I was reasonably confident with my control over my fire. Nina and Stella were learning with me. Stella's kids loved that she could light candles with a wave of her hand. Her family thought she hung the moon. And her husband came in handy when we had to deal with Myrna's death.

Initially Stella was going to keep him in the dark about her magic, but as easy as it seemed to come to her, she couldn't keep from using telekinesis to grab her coffee mug or the toothpaste. The first time it happened Todd accepted her denial and acknowledged he was tired. The second time he refused to back down and she came clean with him. I didn't blame her and in the end, it was to our benefit.

"Will I be able to do that, as well?" Stella set her spoon down and pulled the leather book she and Mythia had made

2

together for her family grimoire, or Book of Shadows as she called it. According to Google, that's what a witch's bible and reference guide was called.

Tarja stood up and stretched with her front legs low to the ground while her back legs and rear end were in the air. *"If you put in the work, yes. You will be able to cast without words. It takes more practice for those who aren't Pleiades. If you had a familiar of your own, it would be easier."*

"Why aren't there any familiars for witches or me at my level?" I realized I hadn't shared that part of the story with Stella when she asked.

"When the Tainted first surfaced, they decimated many. They focused on familiars first and stole their energy. It got them out of the way and left the witches vulnerable. Eventually, we stopped going to Stuleros. It was too dangerous, and then the nightmare ghosts invaded our realm, and no one felt safe there," Tarja responded before I could.

I rubbed my temple. There was so much to unpack in that statement, and I had business proposals to go over. I should ask for clarification. "You mentioned some of that before, but what the heck is Stuleros?"

Stella held up a hand before Tarja explained more. "And, what can we do to make it safe for you to go back? I want a familiar of my own. Most witches do and would be willing to help make that happen."

A weight seemed to settle over Tarja, although it wasn't obvious when you looked at her. I picked up on it because of our connection. *"Stuleros is the realm where familiars go to share information, hang out, and procreate. Only familiars could access it until the Tainted started killing us. That's when the nightmares started showing up. They cling to the realm and chase us. Without the safe haven, Stuleros provided us, it's not safe to leave the protection of our witches and share information, let alone procreate."*

3

Stella tapped her lip. "So, we need to clear out Stuleros for you guys."

"And make sure the Tainted can't get back inside to corrupt the plane again," I added.

Nana waved her spoon and flung pumpkin guts and seeds on Tsekani, who was sitting next to her at the island. "Are there any male familiars you can get it on with, Tarja? Without that, the whole endeavor is pointless."

I laughed and choked when I heard Tarja's purr in my head. "Oh my God, there is. Who is he, and who is his Pleiades? I've not met any of the others yet."

Tarja rolled her eyes which was a disturbing phenomenon on a cat. *"There are three male familiars. Zeph, Vergu, and Ense. I would love nothing more than for witches to once again get familiars. Still, it is not safe in Stuleros, and we have not been able to bring any outsiders with us to the realm."*

"What about if mom astral projected to you when you entered Stuleros?"

I frowned at my teenaged daughter. "I barely managed to project my astral body downstairs last time I tried it."

My mom laid her hand over mine. "That doesn't mean you can't do it, sweetheart. I told you before you still think so much like us mundies."

"Mollie is right. In many ways, the fact that you have such a strong connection to the human world is a huge benefit to the magical world. We've lost sight of it completely, and taking their view into consideration has impacted how we behave for the better. But, in terms of your magic, it's a detriment. You won't be harmed by letting yourself go," Layla interjected.

A knock at the door interrupted our conversation. My mom left to answer it and returned with Brody in tow. Tsekani's face lit up when he saw his boyfriend, but Brody barely cracked a smile. I kept my eyes trained on the guy.

If he and Tseki were in love, he should be happier to see him.

I tried not to let my experience with Miles impact my judgment of others, but it was difficult. Brody was gorgeous, by any standard, and there was something about him that reminded me of Miles. I just didn't know what it was.

"Is it four already?" Tsekani stood up and took his tools to the sink.

Brody lifted one shoulder. "I'm early."

Tsekani rinsed his spoon and knife then washed his hands. "We can head out now if you want."

Brody walked over to Tseki's pumpkin and frowned. "What are you doing?"

"We're carving pumpkins." Nana's tone said that should be obvious.

"You know it originally started in Ireland and Scotland to ward off evil spirits?" Stella must be referring to her Google knowledge again. The internet had surprisingly accurate information. I assumed it was all a joke, but that was how everyone shared information, even in the magical community. "I know that's the reason I'm doing an extra one this year. I've met these evil spirits first hand."

"Perhaps we should get a few more," my mom suggested.

I laughed. Life had been relatively peaceful for the past few months. Halloween seemed like as good a time as any to drop the hammer on us. "Does it actually work?"

Tarja's scratchy hacking sound echoed in my head. "*It might work to frighten some Fae, but evil doesn't care about scary faces carved into gourds.*"

Mythia held up a finger. "For the record, they don't frighten pixies. We had Voron for a king. There's nothing scarier than him."

I begged to differ. I hadn't met him, but he'd have to be horrendous to be worse than Myrna had been. "Good thing I

5

have wards to keep out those with malicious intentions. No one can approach us if they have a nefarious plan in mind."

"How are the lower-level demons getting through if your wards are all that good?" My jaw dropped at Brody's question, and Tsekani jerked next to him, then chuckled to cover his apparent surprise.

"We believe they have been inside since the veil was opened," Tsekani explained.

My hackles were up, and I struggled to keep from throwing out a biting retort. The truth was, Brody wasn't part of my inner circle. I viewed him as an outsider and thus didn't trust him. And, it wasn't fair of me.

In his shoes, I would likely be curious about how things worked. Especially if my boyfriend was the one fighting evil creatures.

"That makes sense," Brody acknowledged. "I guess I would have expected them to be thrown out by the magic or something unless there were weak spots in the perimeter."

Layla stabbed her knife through the middle of her pumpkin in an exceptionally aggressive move. "We have the perimeter monitored to ensure no potions or crystals are eating through the barrier Phoebe cast. It's a large property, but we have enough numbers. Don't worry, your boyfriend will be alright."

Nana scowled. "You do realize he's *Loong*, right?" My forehead furrowed, and my eyes widened. "What?" Nana asked.

"You know what kind of dragon he is?" I asked.

Nana huffed. "Stella isn't the only one that can use Google."

Our laughter was interrupted by another knock at the door. Perhaps there'd be another missing ghost to find. I left the kitchen and opened the door to find a frazzled woman standing on my porch.

"Thank god someone is home. I need help." She was a wreck. Her clothes were as dirty as her brown hair. It was knotted and had dirt and leaves sticking out of it. She also had wide, frantic hazel eyes, and her complexion was pale. It put me on alert at once.

"What happened? What do you need help with?" I moved aside and gestured for her to enter the house. She was agitated and kept looking over her shoulder. My gut told me she wasn't a trap. I didn't get an evil vibe from her. Although she felt different from what I had encountered so far.

"Someone is after me. She felt wrong. I think she was Tainted."

I led her to the kitchen, where everyone was gathered. She shrank back and hesitated. "It's okay. We are all family here. No one is going to hurt you. Start from the beginning and tell me why you think a Tainted is after you. Wait. Sorry, we should start with introductions. I'm Phoebe."

At the mention of Tainted, I went straight into detective mode. I needed to remember how to have actual conversations. I briefly introduced her to everyone, and Mythia grabbed a water bottle and handed it to the woman.

"I'm Selene Digby, and I'm pretty sure I was killed."

Gasps filled the room, and instinctively, I reached out and touched her shoulder. I knew she was alive because Mythia had handed her a bottle of water. Plus, she wasn't the exact bluish figure as Evanora, who was hovering in the corner of the ceiling watching us.

The ghost had helped me a while back with finding a missing spirit and had been slowly integrating into the family, so to speak. I lifted one eyebrow at her and motioned her forward.

Evanora dropped down and paused in front of me. "She's not a ghost. But she's not alive. I can't see her aura like the rest of you."

7

My mom put her hand to her chest and crossed to Selene. "What does that mean? Does she need a doctor? Perhaps she's bleeding internally or something."

"I don't think auras are based on injuries. Why do you say you think you were killed?" I scanned her and saw no obvious evidence of injury. And there was no blood on her filthy clothes.

Selene's hand went to her side. "I was leaving work late and walking to my car when some guy grabbed me and dragged me to a nearby alley. I almost got away from him, but he pulled out a knife. I remember the pain of the blade slicing through my chest. I remember a three-headed dog, and I swore I was surrounded by dead supernatural creatures in the Underworld. Still, I woke up with a Tainted witch laughing gleefully. She kept trying to get me to do stuff for her. At first, I was compelled to break into her ex-boyfriend's house. It's all confusing, but somehow, I managed to run away when she sent me to try and get to her ex's new girl-friend. At least I assumed that's who the guy and girl were. I couldn't see any other reason she wanted to hurt them like that."

Tarja jumped off the island and prowled closer. "*Are you struggling with the compulsion to complete a task or return to your maker?*"

Selene shook her head. "At first, I wanted to go back because I wasn't sure where I was or where I should go. All I knew was I craved meat. I almost ate a dead deer on the side of the road which is doubly traumatizing for me because I'm a vegan. After that, I wandered around, not really seeing anything. I was terrified and prayed for some help. After that, something told me to head toward Camden. Now, I don't ever want to go back. I just want to understand what happened."

"She smells like decay," Brody blurted. "She definitely died."

Maybe I wasn't too hard on him after all. He could have told us without Selene present. The poor woman was shaking like a leaf. Every shifter in the room flared their noses and tilted their heads. I gently grabbed her hand and pressed my fingers, checking for a pulse. "She has a pulse. How is that possible if she died?"

"I'm sorry, Selene, but he's right. You did die. The witch that was there when you woke up brought you back as a ghoul. The process of bringing someone back restarts their heart and restores their life, for the most part. It takes a powerful witch or an average witch drawing on an extremely powerful location. The reason Evanora can't see your aura is that your soul isn't attached to your body."

"So, I'm like a zombie? That's why I wanted the deer?" Selene's voice wobbled. It was clear she was terrified. I wasn't sure why I expected a ghoul to be a violent creature that went around killing others. It was apparent that wasn't how Selene was at all.

"You're not a zombie. You crave flesh. Meat. But you won't kill for it, and you might even prefer it cooked. My guess is you were weak at the time. The biggest issue for you is that you are vulnerable to possession. I'll do some research into how we can help. I've never had experience with one of your kind."

Mythia held a plate of ribs out to Selene. "If meat is what you need, this should help you feel better."

Selene took the plate from the pixie with a smile. "Thank you." She lifted one and took a bite, humming in appreciation. "So, I'm not evil? That's all I could think about. That somehow the Tainted witch managed to Turn me into some perverted version of the witch I used to be."

Looked like the calm had shattered. My first thought was one of relief. I constantly worried about what Zaleria and the other Tainted would do next. Knowing was far better. Now we could protect against their attacks.

"You aren't a bad witch," I reassured Selene before I addressed everyone else. "We need to be on alert for other ghouls. My guess is Zaleria is creating creatures that will do her bidding, so we are likely to face others."

Stella dropped her spoon into her pumpkin. "Looks like we need to hit the books again."

I nodded my head. Her eagerness to learn was infectious and made every new discovery fun. I grabbed my reading glasses and followed her to the library. No time like the present. I needed to know if it was safe to have a ghoul eating ribs in my house.

CHAPTER 2

*M*y sixteen-year-old daughter took this magical world in stride and with more than a bit of excitement which was the best blessing I could have been given. "Before you guys go off researching ghouls and the magic of them, have you considered looking her up and seeing what happened to her? It might give you a clue about where this Zaleria is located."

I looked from her to Stella then Layla. "That's a good idea. In the least, we can get confirmation that you are right about what happened to you, Selene. Tsekani, you can go on your date with Brody. You don't need to stick around for this."

I had no idea how Selene's brain functioned at all after her death. Yet, there was no denying she recalled who she was and most likely her last moments. It was an impossibility I couldn't truly wrap my mind around.

Tsekani nodded his head and grabbed Brody's hand. "Alright, if you're sure. I'll have my cell phone with me." To my surprise, Brody didn't seem to want to leave. I didn't understand the guy at all.

Nina jumped off her stool and raced out of the room. She

was back a few seconds later with her laptop. She turned it on, and as soon as it was booted up, she opened her internet search engine, and her fingers were flying over the keyboard.

"Looks like Selene Digby was found murdered two weeks ago in Salem, Massachusetts. Is that where you are from?" How had she gotten all the way to Camden? It was a significant distance to travel without a vehicle. And, why was she here in my house? I didn't want to be responsible for a ghoul that was attached to an evil entity.

"Do you think this could be someone other than Zaleria?" I couldn't see her sending this traumatized woman after me. Unless I was missing something. "Or could she have implanted an order in Selene to kill me in my sleep? Otherwise, I don't see why she would send the ghoul here."

Stella sucked air through her teeth. "I don't think we know enough about ghouls. You do have a good point, though. Zaleria has sent demons and the Tainted after you. This seems like a step back. Perhaps, you hurt her when you killed Myrna."

"I have yet to discover the true identity of this Zaleria, so I cannot say from personal knowledge of her. The question is valid, and considering Selene in terms of what we know about the Dark One, it seems unlikely she is behind this. From what I know, a ghoul must be possessed to be controlled."

Layla dropped several books on the island. Everyone took one and started paging through them-even Selene. I had a book on supernatural creatures. There was no index or table of contents in the book. And, it wasn't printed in a way I was used to seeing, although it was printed and not hand-written.

Each page had an illustration above a name followed by descriptions. There was one on imps. They were tiny demonic creatures with red skin, horns, and a tail. They thrived on causing chaos and liked to play pranks. They weren't particularly bloodthirsty, but their antics were often violent and harmed their targets.

The passage on ghosts indicated they were strong spirits of magical beings that lingered on this plane. Mundies could become ghosts but most often because they suffered violent deaths. They needed to experience a traumatic death that anchored their spirit to this realm.

Ghouls were magical beings that only a powerful witch could bring back from the dead. Their souls are left in limbo where it is vulnerable to being consumed, and their bodies are defenseless against possession. Their consciousness is returned to their body, and they are alive, in that they eat, drink and sleep. And their hearts beat. The book didn't mention that, but I felt Selene's pulse.

It cautioned against starving one or denying it meat. To do so would cause them to become crazed. And they could be brought back in various stages of decomposition. I was very grateful Selene hadn't been dead long. I doubt I could stomach looking at a ghoul missing part of its cheek like in the illustration.

"There's nothing in this one about a ghoul being a violent or aggressive creature. It's vulnerable to possession, so if a demon took charge of her, I could see it going on a rampage with her body," I announced after reading my passage.

Nana pointed to her book. "In this one, it says they're rare because of the energy it takes to create one. I guess it leaves the creator weak for some time, and few are willing to take that risk."

Stella waved her book in front of her face. "This one says the witch that made the ghoul can impose her will on it without needing to possess it. We need to find this witch so she can't cause problems for us."

"That explains how she made me do her bidding. She was erratic and pissed," Selene said.

13

"How did you find your way here? You mentioned being driven to us."

Selene set her book down and grabbed another rib from the plate. She'd eaten half of them. Thank god she didn't attack them and snarl while she ate. "I was lost, frightened, and prayed for help. It was after that I got the nudge in this direction. When I reached the town limits, I followed the power here. I knew my best bet of getting help would be with the most powerful witch in the area. No one else would be able to do anything for me."

My chest tightened. I had no way of helping her. "Has anyone come across anything on how to do something for a ghoul?"

A rock formed in my stomach at the heads shaking from side to side. My new client proved to be more challenging to assist than finding a missing ghost and sewing machine.

"I just got another listing out of town. This one is for a witch. I can ask her if she knows anything about ghouls." Stella's real estate business was booming. She'd been right to pursue paranormal listings.

I considered her offer and shook my head. "I guess it couldn't hurt. I just don't want the witches in the area thinking I'm weak. That would be counterproductive. And make me an even bigger target."

"What about calling Fiona? She's a powerful witch, too, right? Maybe she knows something and can give you some advice," my mom suggested.

Fiona might actually be able to help me. Certainly, between her, Violet and Aislinn, they would have some answers. "That's perfect, mom. Months ago, she mentioned bringing her grandmother's ghost back before bringing her back. She might know something."

After calculating it was only a little after nine at night, I grabbed my cell from my purse. At the same time, Mythia set the aluminum stand on the island. I hit the FaceTime button for Fiona and put the phone in the cradle.

"Phoebe! So good to see you. How are things going? Did you get that potion down?" Fiona's smiling face filled the screen. I recalled how melancholic she'd been for years after her husband, Tim, died. Ever since she moved to England and unlocked her magic and claimed her position as Guardian for the Fae portal, my friend had been happier than I'd seen her in over a decade.

"I'm good. We were carving pumpkins when I got a new case. It's one I hope you can help me with." I bit my lip, praying she had some information.

"You know I'm always happy to help, but let me get Grams and Sebastian. They might be able to offer some help, as well." Fiona looked beyond her screen and waved a hand. "Bas, Grams, can you come in the living room? Phoebe's on the phone and needs help."

Grams' silver hair and bright eyes entered the side of the screen. "Hi, Phoebe. You look better than the last time I saw you."

"Thanks. There are no lingering injuries from the fight with Myrna."

Bas's gruff features towered above Fiona as he inclined his head but didn't say anything. His hands landed on Fiona's shoulders. I envied the way she melted into him. "How can we help you this time?"

I cleared my wayward thoughts. It wouldn't help to think about the confusing son of Hades. "About an hour ago, a ghoul knocked on my door. I have no idea how to help her or what to do aside from feeding her meat."

Grams gasped, and Fiona's eyes flew open wide. Sebastian's fingers tightened on Fiona's shoulders. What was up with that? Was Grams a ghoul?

Fiona took a deep breath. "Remember when I said I brought Grams back from the dead?"

I iclined my head. Mythia landed on my shoulder while everyone else crowded around me to see the phone. "Yeah. You said you brought her ghost back first. What about it?"

"I brought her back as a ghoul. I had no idea what I was doing and didn't do it intentionally. We had no idea what I'd done until Thanos told us what she was." Fiona shook her head from side to side.

"You look good for a dead broad," Nana observed.

Grams chuckled. "I feel better than I have in a long time. And I don't have the aches and pains much like I used to."

"I'd be okay with that. Especially if I had better bladder control. Peeing myself every time I laugh or sneeze is for the birds."

Everyone laughed at Nana. I had to do an emergency Kegel, hoping to keep from wetting myself a little. I had to agree with Nana. I'd give that up and the rare hot flashes I was beginning to experience.

"You can help me with Selene, then. What do I do for her?" Perhaps this case wouldn't be all that hard after all.

"You need to keep her away from demons. She can be possessed. Grams had an incident with an imp. It wasn't pretty, but we were able to deal with it without hurting Grams in the process."

My heart dropped. "I read something about that. How can I protect her from possession without having to be with her twenty-four-seven?"

Fiona shook her head from side to side. "I'm not sure. Thanos told me I had to bond her soul to her body, so that's what I did. But I'd already called her soul back when I summoned her ghost. And, all of it was done by accident."

Grams patted her arm. "I cast a spell to bind my spirit to

this realm. I knew someone wanted me dead, and I didn't want to be here until Fiona was ready for me."

"She wouldn't have been able to keep her mouth shut and allow Fiona time to come to grips with her power and role." I blinked at Sebastian. He looked angry, but there was an undeniable hint of affection in his tone.

Fiona's grandmother wagged a finger at him. "You're lucky I wasn't around. If I had been, Fiona never would have turned to you for help, and you wouldn't have discovered she was the love of your life for decades, as stubborn as you are."

Fiona laughed while Sebastian shrugged his shoulders. "What does she remember?"

I turned to Selene and drew her forward. "This is Selene," Selene told them what she recalled about her death and after.

"I'm not sure what to do when her soul seems to be in the Underworld. There might be a way to bring it through and tether it to her body. I can walk you through that process if your familiar finds a way for you to summon it to this realm," Fiona offered.

"Is there anything I should be aware of about ghouls aside from they can be possessed and they require meat?" The call hadn't been a total bust. At least I got to see and talk to Fiona again.

Sebastian shifted, his large shoulders moving behind Fiona's head. He was good-looking and the complete opposite of Tim, but he was perfect for my best friend. "If she is possessed by a demon, it could get past your wards. Ghouls have no soul and aren't deemed a danger, so they wouldn't trigger any protections. Wards react to what is in a being's soul. Their undead status will obscure their passenger." That explained how Selene managed to make it to my door. I hadn't thought about it earlier because she was very clearly terrified. She didn't make a move against me, so I didn't question it.

"I would think the demon would be detected. I can't say I like that they could slip by if they inhabit a ghoul."

Nina shook her head. "I'm not surprised. Demons have snuck through all the time.'

"They've been lower-level demons whose souls and power aren't often enough to trigger the protections. It makes sense that the ghoul could confuse the ward if it was possessed by a higher-level demon. It can't solve problems or make adjustments. It has a set parameter and works within that."

Grams leaned closer to the phone. "Is that your familiar talking?"

I glanced down at Tarja and picked her up. "Yes. This is Tarja. I had no idea she could speak into your minds, too. I thought it was a proximity thing." England was an entire ocean away.

"I think 'line of sight' means she can include us," Fiona's grandmother reasoned.

"Isidora is right about that. I can include them because I can see them through the phone."

Fiona watched Tarja closely. "She doesn't even move her mouth. I want a familiar."

I laughed. "I couldn't imagine doing this without Tarja. Right now, only Pleiades have them."

"But we've talked about finding a way for Tarja to get her groove on and start procreating. We'll let you know if anything comes of it," Nana added.

I laughed, needing to change the subject. I didn't want word to get out about that if we couldn't come up with a viable plan. "That's a conversation for another day. There will be no trips for you without one of us with you, Selene. I don't mean to keep you captive, but we can't risk you being possessed. I don't think Zaleria made you, but she will definitely use you if she can."

"If a demon possesses you and you are killed, your soul

ceases to exist. It will be blown to bits in limbo." Selene flinched and paled considerably with Fiona's grandmother's words.

I grabbed Selene's hands and squeezed them. "Don't worry. We will make sure that doesn't happen." I focused back on the phone. "Thank you for all the information. I will definitely call you if we find a way to bring Selene's soul from limbo. Aidoneus might be able to help, as well. If Thanos knew about ghouls, he might as well."

"Be careful, Phoebe. The magic that creates a ghoul is questionable. I know Thanos was surprised I wasn't Tainted. I'm not sure if my Fae side saved me. I didn't actually cast the spell intending for Grams to become one. I missed her and wanted her back enough that it hijacked my enchantment. Whoever created Selene could be as Tainted as they come."

A smile creased my face. "We discussed that fact earlier. I have Layla here and a large population of pixies, plus were-wolves and a dragon."

Sebastian's expression shifted. Not by a whole lot, but the minute change was visible. "Pixies usually don't live together. Do you guys have a queen?" The last part was directed at Mythia.

Mythia's wings fluttered and blew my hair away from my cheek. "Daethie is our leader. Most look to her as our queen, but she refuses to take the title."

"Why wouldn't she want to be queen?" Nina asked.

Sebastian responded before Mythia was able. "When Vodor took the Fae throne, the pixies dispersed and hid after he killed their queen. He was threatened by anyone ruling aside from him."

"And Daethie feels it would be a betrayal to our fallen queen to assume the title," Mythia added.

"I love talking to you guys. I learn something new every time we get on the phone, but I won't keep you any longer. I know it's late over there." Everyone said their goodbyes, and I ended the call.

I needed ibuprofen and a big glass of wine before I went back to researching. I needed to know as much as possible. Selene's weaknesses were significant and terrifying. And there might be more weaknesses I didn't know about ghouls.

CHAPTER 3

"*J* got it," I called out as I ran from Layla before she could tackle me for a third time. Sweat covered my body, and my lime green tank top stuck to my skin in places. Layla insisted on having training sessions a few days a week. Luckily, something usually pulled me away after thirty to forty-five minutes.

I was breathing hard when I yanked the door open. The sexy smirk and bright sapphire blue eyes made my heart beat even faster at the same time butterflies filled my stomach. Aidoneus ran a hand through his messy black hair as he scanned me from head to toe.

I wished I'd allowed my mom to answer. Then I could have dashed into the laundry room and changed clothes. Instead, I stood there, a sweaty mess. "Aidon. I didn't know you were back in town." That was eloquent. I turned and found Layla silently laughing at me.

"I just got back. I didn't mean to interrupt. I can come back later." He didn't sound very sorry. His tone carried hints of amusement and desire.

I was reasonably certain it was desire, anyway. I'd spent

decades married and ignorant before the blinders were ripped painfully from my eyes. Then I'd gotten a crash course in how to identify when a man was attracted to a woman and being subtle about it.

"It's alright. Layla and I were training, but now's a good time for a break. Come in." I stalked forward and snatched the towel from Layla's hand, wiping my face and neck as I continued into the kitchen to grab some hydration. Maybe one that would give me a boost. I hadn't slept well the last few nights with a ghoul in the house.

"Can I get you something to drink?" I paused at the fridge and snagged a grape energy drink.

Aidoneus wrapped his arms around my waist and took the can from my hand. I gripped his shoulders before his lips descended on mine. His kiss was insistent and instantly turned my blood to lava.

His arms enveloped me and tugged me against his hard body. I wanted to object because I was all sweaty, and then his tongue slid into my mouth. As it tangled with mine and my mind became focused on one thought, I warred with the desire to tug him upstairs into my bedroom.

The past few months, we'd shared several stolen kisses, and every time the need between us rose higher. There would come a point soon when neither of us would be able to stop from going to the next level. My body shook from arousal and nerves. I was once again a giddy teenager when I thought about sneaking around with him to get naked.

A whistle and catcall made me jump and break away from him. My chest was heaving up and down as I caught my breath. Funny how I hadn't needed to breathe a second ago.

"You didn't have to stop on my account," Nana said as she shuffled into the kitchen. Not the best place to make out. "I was enjoying the show. I came to get some key lime pie if there's any left. Good to see you, Aidoneus. I was going to ask if you were here to help with the ghoul, but I can see you're here for my granddaughter."

Aidon lifted one eyebrow with a questioning look on his face. I waved it away and grabbed the pie for Nana. "You've been gone for a few weeks. It's been busy."

Mythia flittered into the kitchen, followed by Layla and Selene, who were both laughing. "Oh, shut up." I hadn't meant to growl at them.

Layla sauntered to the fridge while I grabbed a plate and got Nana a piece of the pie. "No need to be grumpy just because Nana vag-blocked you."

Aidoneus had cracked the energy drink open and started choking on a mouthful when she said that. His face turned red, and he coughed. It made him undeniably human for a split second, and I forgot he was, in reality, a god.

Mythia sprayed cleaner on the floor where the drink landed. "You will not ever have sex on my counters. We eat in here. No one wants their food touching counters where your ass has touched."

My face heated, and I wanted to crawl into a hole. Time to set the record straight. "No need to worry about that. We aren't having sex."

"Yet," Nana interjected. "I bet the son of Hades has some moves. You could have done worse. Actually, you have done worse."

Selene's jaw dropped open then snapped shut as her gaze shifted from Nana to Aidon. "You're not going to smite them, are you?"

Aidoneus chuckled and shook his head. "I wouldn't dream of it. Everything Amelia said is accurate. I've come to appreciate the unique outlook of those living at Nimaha. You need to be careful, though. I won't hesitate to smite you if you present a risk to anyone in this house. You're not carrying a Dark passenger right now, but that could change."

It was odd to hear Aidon say Nana's name. It sounded as if they were friends which only reminded me of our massive age difference.

Mythia set the containers she was holding on the counter. "Selene is the ghoul, as you obviously sensed. We're looking for a way to help her that doesn't involve destroying her."

I nodded my head. "You wouldn't happen to have a way to get her soul out of limbo, would you?"

Aidoneus took another sip of the energy drink then handed it to me. "Her soul is in a section of limbo, or the Fields of Asphodel, that is beyond my reach. All souls go to the Fields when they arrive. When a ghoul is made, it goes to a protected section that was created by Hebe."

"Who is Hebe, and what are her powers? Is there a way I can sneak past and grab Selene's soul?" I couldn't allow her to be killed. I couldn't imagine a worse fate than ceasing to exist altogether.

Aidoneus sat on the island next to Nana. It was the first time he'd done so. Usually, he stood around, never quite relaxing or becoming one of us. "Hebe is underestimated because she spent centuries as a slave of sorts on Mount Olympus, serving them nectar or preparing her brother, Ares's chariot. She's not all rainbows and kittens. She obtained eternal youth when she created her prison for kidnapped souls and shared it with her husband. Neither she nor Heracles wants to give it up, so they don't like letting anyone out."

I shivered at the thought. It was easy for me to forget who Aidoneus really was. He rarely talked about his family. He grew up in a place I believed was only a myth. And his family had the power to do things few ever truly contemplated.

"So, it's hopeless. We will need to make sure demons don't get to you, Selene. With Aidoneus around, they tend to stay away. Those that take the risk won't get past Layla or

Tsekani." Giving up wasn't in my nature, but I knew when I was beaten. I had no way to take on a goddess.

The way Selene's shoulders slumped and her face fell hit me like a two-ton truck. A fist closed around my heart, and a lead weight settled in my stomach. Selene was an innocent woman living her life, trying to use her magic for good. When she shared that she was a social worker and had used spells to help kids being harmed, I wanted to rant at the universe. I wanted to do it again, but for another reason altogether.

Aidon nudged my shoulder with his. "Don't give up hope just yet. I'll ask around and do some research in my father's library. But first, I have an issue I'd like to discuss."

Tarja prowled in at that moment and jumped onto the stool next to Aidoneus. My familiar was comfortable around the son of Hades, which was good because I hoped he would remain a regular fixture around here.

My mom was smiling when she entered next. "Well, hello, Aidoneus. Good to see you came to help with Selene. The poor dear needs her soul, and the sooner, the better."

"You missed the show, dear. He came to make out with Phoebe," Nana informed my mother. My face flamed brighter than the Olympic torch, and I fought the urge to run from the house.

I sucked in a breath and plowed on despite my utter embarrassment. "We can talk about the kissing later." It was better to get that out there. My mother and grandmother would never stop teasing me if I tried to ignore it. "Aidoneus was just telling us he's here to discuss something, and it sounded important."

My mom sobered and immediately crossed to help Mythia. She grabbed a knife and the vegetables. "Diced or julienned?"

"Rough chop. We're making stew," Mythia replied. "You were saying?"

Aidoneus turned the drink can between his fingers. "I've been looking for a way to keep lower-level demons from passing through the veil. As you all know, it's easier for witches to summon a weaker being from the Underworld. Well, turns out Fae can wield the same magic. That's not to say the Dark One we're looking for is necessarily Fae. There is no way to seal the veil entirely. It would close the doors to souls altogether. And my agents and I have no way of tracking them when they cross."

A lump formed in my throat. "Did you find a way to track them now?" I prayed there was an easy solution that didn't involve Aidoneus needing to travel worldwide chasing assholes brought through the veil.

I was in deep trouble, despite the warnings I'd issued repeatedly in my head. He was the son of Hades with a job and home in the Underworld. There was no future for us, no matter how much I wanted it.

Aidon shook his head and gulped the last of the energy drink he had picked up. "There's no way to monitor every inch of the veil. It's too big, and the power required would kill the god or goddess that attempted it. My father told me the mere idea was absurd, and I didn't need to worry about something beneath my role."

I needed another drink. And a break from looking at him. My gut churned with the certainty he was going to say he was leaving for good. Angry at myself for wanting to cry, I snatched a citrus soda and popped the top.

"What do we need to prepare for when you're gone?" I was proud my voice didn't wobble once.

"There's something we need to do together if you'd let me finish." There was an edge to his voice that made the lizard part of my brain shout for me to run.

"Sorry. I made an assumption I shouldn't have." I used to try and cover or ignore my mistakes. After what Miles did, I vowed I would always own my shit. Especially if there was any chance of a future. I wanted open and honest communication from the start.

A smile creased his face. "That's the first time I've ever heard a woman say they're wrong."

"That's because I'm a rare and beautiful flower." Everyone laughed when I said that.

"Even rarer than the Middlemist red. Two of those flowers exist in the world, and there is only one of you." I wanted to melt into Aidoneus's arms. Miles didn't ply me with romantic sentiment. In hindsight, it should have warned me away from him.

Nana sighed and clapped Aidoneus on the shoulder. "Before you start locking lips again, what did you come to tell us."

Aidoneus shook his head and sat straight. "What we need to do is create a Hellmouth."

I immediately thought of Buffy the Vampire Slayer. Over twenty years ago, the show about the teenage cheerleader whose school was positioned above a Hellmouth was popular. "You mean like they had in Buffy?"

My mom and Nana laughed, but no one else in the room reacted. "You know the TV show where the main character is a Vampire Slayer?"

Aidoneus shook his head. "I know the show. It was ridiculous. Vampires don't turn to ash when you stake them. And you know how bloody it is to kill demons. But, the description of a Hellmouth was fairly accurate. Especially in the last season. A Hellmouth acts as a gateway to the Underworld. It has only been used a few times throughout history because it takes so much energy to maintain. Few gods want to leave themselves that vulnerable."

"But you're willing to do that? How exactly does this work?" I drank the rest of the soda and tossed it into the recycling along with the empty energy drink.

"I need to cast a modified reinforcement spell. It's like adding a layer of titanium mesh beneath the veil anchored at as many Hellmouths as possible. That will make it impossible for anything to get through any location aside from the Hellmouth."

I practically jumped for joy. Most of the problems we'd encountered came from demons. If we could remove that threat, not only would my town be safer, but Zaleria would also lose her greatest weapon against me. "We can stop demons from crossing the veil? How can I help?"

Aidoneus chuckled, the deep sound rumbling through me. I had to fight the shiver of pleasure. I didn't need my family to see how much he affected me. "I need your help, but it will not stop all demons from getting through. I need space in the area to anchor the Hellmouth and your help in anchoring it. I theorize if a powerful witch such as a *nicotisa* backed by a large coven or a Pleiades bonds to it along with the agent assigned, we can avoid draining too much energy from either of them. In fact, I doubt the expenditure would be felt. I can't be certain since it hasn't been done before."

"Where would you be anchoring this gateway?"

"Ideally on the property adjacent to yours. It's close enough to you and makes it easy to monitor the seal."

My heart plummeted. That didn't mean he would be here to help. "And, you'll be in the Underworld taking care of things from there?"

He shook his head. "No. The mesh will be between this realm and mine, so I will need to live here. Next door, if you have no objections."

"You're not having a mid-life crisis and joining a noisy

death metal band, are you? I'd need to make sure you were much further if that's your ultimate goal."

He threw back his head and laughed. "No bands, promise. But you need to be sure. This isn't going to be an easy task. And, we will need at least one more location in the world, or it won't work. Do you think another Pleiades will be willing to play host?"

"I don't know any of the other Pleiades." I had seen their information in a file on Hattie's computer, but I wasn't going to call up and say, 'Hey, I know you don't know me, but want to host a Hellmouth?'

"What about Thanos? Phoebe's best friend, Fiona, is a powerful witch. I suspect she's a nicotisa. And so is Fiona's friend, Violet. Although, there is more to her than I understand. Perhaps they can do it. If your friend is in fact one of the nicotisa then you must keep this a secret. Her life would be in danger if word got out. Her power can be stolen, unlike yours, Phoebe."

Aidoneus rubbed a hand over his face. "I have faith that no one in this room would say a thing to endanger a friend. I've met Violet. She's a witch-phoenix hybrid. You might be right about Fiona. I know the three in Cottlehill share a connection. If Fiona is a *nicotisa*, that would explain why Violet felt different. I don't know if she's powerful enough, but we can talk to Thanos and the witches."

Nana tilted her head and pinned Aidoneus with her stare. "You never clarified the issue of demons crossing over. Will they still be able to get through?"

I'd never seen Aidon flinch before. I knew how alarming it was to be under Nana's scrutiny. "Yes. Demons will always find a way to cross over, but now it will be far more difficult. Lower-level demons won't be able to slip past the barrier undeterred. The mesh cannot bar everything, or the exchange of energy necessary for life to continue and the balance to be maintained will be destroyed. If that happens, bad shit happens."

"What does opening a Hellmouth mean for you? There's more you aren't telling me. And, what does your father say about this?" I needed to know everything before I agreed.

Aidoneus sucked in a breath. "That's a longer conversation, and I'm hungry. Can we eat before continuing this conversation?"

I nodded my head while a large boulder settled in my throat. I couldn't say anything yet, so I helped make garlic bread. The act of cooking provided a comforting familiarity. I had done all the cooking throughout the twenty years I was married and had taken full advantage of the break my mother and Mythia offered.

CHAPTER 4

*N*ana extended her hand toward me. "Pass me the garlic, Phoebe. There isn't enough on my bread."

I picked up the serving dish full of the cooked, crushed garlic. "I put a ton on the loaves before I toasted it."

She took the ceramic from my hand with a shake of her head. "I've told you a thousand times to add more. You shouldn't be able to see the holes beneath the spread."

Nana would have gas and bad breath when she was done eating, but she didn't care. I hoped I didn't give a rip at her age, either. "You're right. I'll add more next time, but you might want to eat an antacid now, so you aren't regretting it later."

"Already did. I'm old, not senile. Did you ever ask Aidoneus about the fame demon? I've held off visiting her bakery like you asked, but I want to go this week." I'd forgotten about the woman until Nana mentioned her.

"What's this about a fame demon? They're tricky creatures. More often than not, you can't trust them. Then there are the ones like Ted that go on killing sprees to gain their fame. I was cleaning up that mess for decades. And, the asshole lives high on the continued adoration he garnered during his time on Earth."

My eyes went wide, and my hand flew to my chest. "Are you saying that the serial killer was a fame demon?" Why had I allowed Marilee to remain in her house? I should have asked about her sooner.

Aidoneus put his spoon down and placed his hand on mine. "You're okay. Yes, most serial killers are fame demons that refuse to work for their energy. But you can't judge them all based on the few. Many take jobs in Hollywood as actors and models, and they're harmless. We keep tabs on them but don't interfere unless they do something to harm mundies. The Underworld is overcrowded, so leaving demons like that alone thins the masses." It made sense that actors and models were demons that thrived on attention. I couldn't imagine tolerating the loss of privacy by becoming famous.

"What other kinds of demons are roaming the Earth with us?" Nina asked around a mouthful.

Nana waved her piece of garlic bread. "I bet that Sally at the Senior Center is a rage demon or something. That woman is happiest when she's fighting and angry."

I laughed. Nana hated Sally with a passion. Something to do with the time she tried to steal grandpa away from grandma. "You need to stop letting that woman upset you. Have they even let you back in the center?"

"Not until next week," my mom interjected.

Aidoneus gave me one of his smiles. "Sally could be a rage demon, but we rarely leave them here. They're too unpredictable. To answer your questions, Nina. The most common ones on Earth are ice demons, fire demons, incubi and succubi, pain demons, blood demons, and mischief demons. Sometimes a nightmare proves to have a stable life, and we allow him to stay. Those tend to live in remote areas and give nightmares to the animals around them."

I glared at Aidon. "You allow Nightmares to stay on Earth? And Pain demons? I get that the Underworld is crowded, but what the hell? Animals don't deserve to suffer from bad dreams. How can you be so callous?"

Had I completely misjudged him? We hadn't spent all that much time together. And I didn't know much about him when it all boiled down. I let his stories about trying to live up to his father's expectations affect me. That and his sexy smiles.

How could I have made out with a guy that saw nothing wrong with allowing a creature to live off of other people's pain? I worked for twenty years as a nurse and saw countless people in agony. I couldn't stomach the thought.

Aidoneus's expression fell before he shut down. "You're thinking is narrow-minded. Just because a creature has *demon* in their title doesn't mean they're evil. I expected better from you. The disgust on your face is offensive and reminds me of the worst days of the civil rights movement in your country. It's appalling to me that my father and I are judged evil when neither of us would dream of assuming what you were like just because you were a certain color or had certain powers."

That stomach ache morphed into full-blown agony. There was an invisible boa constrictor around my chest that was having a heyday trying to milk all the blood from my body. I'd offended him.

I opened my mouth to apologize, and he held up a hand. "No. Pain demons thrive on pain, yes. But that doesn't mean they cause it. Many have become successful doctors."

"I think your ex-husband is one of those demons," Nana interjected. "Only, he isn't one of the nice ones."

Aidoneus chuckled, and I smiled to see some of the

tension leave his body. "He's not a demon yet. I checked after I met Phoebe. No offense, Nina. I know he's your father."

I fell for the son of Hades a little more in that second and realized he'd been right to scold me. I shouldn't jump to conclusions because of what they were. Nina shrugged her shoulders. "Thanks. I don't like my father. He treated my mom horribly my entire life. There have been so many days where my brother and I worried we were going to be like him because we have half of his genes."

"There's not a chance of that. You've shown me what a thoughtful and caring young woman you are. Just like your mom."

"I shouldn't have jumped to conclusions like that, Aidon. I was reacting to the idea that it didn't matter if animals were given nightmares."

Aidoneus grabbed my free hand. "Most animals don't dream like humans, so it doesn't harm them. I want to clarify the demons that live here aren't harming people. Blood demons work in mortuaries where they aren't doing any harm by ingesting the blood they remove. There are about a hundred that are cardiologists where they can use their ability to manipulate the heart. Pain demons often work in oncology due to the maximum benefit for them, but also so they can use their power to block nerves and save patients from the worst of the pain."

"This is all so fascinating, and I feel like a fool. Thank you for reminding me to keep an open mind. I thought I'd been pretty good about it since becoming a witch. No one's perfect, and I just got a big dose of humility." I looked up at him through my lashes. I wanted to ask his forgiveness but didn't say anything given our audience. Nana and my mom had a thing about asking for forgiveness. The last thing I wanted was to have that injected into this discussion.

Aidoneus cupped my cheek. "Your ability to admit your

HELLMOUTH & HOT FLASHES

mistakes is one of the things that draws me to you. And is a lesson I never learned in life. I would have argued with you had I been in your position. Your humanity is a breath of fresh air."

Nina got up and rinsed her dishes before she put them in the dishwasher. "Alright, dinner is done. Now, will you tell me about Hellmouths?"

I laughed at her eager expression. I stood and grabbed Aidoneus's bowl, then took his and mine to the sink while he told Nina about the Hellmouth. Her eyes got wider and wider as he spoke.

"So, this is going to be a permanent portal to the Underworld? Is it one that humans can accidentally fall into? I'd hate for my friends to accidentally drop to hell because we were out there having a few drinks and not paying attention. And before you freak out, mom. No, I don't plan on doing that at sixteen, but I will one day. Although, we would like to have a Halloween party here."

I hugged her from behind. "I'll be sure and have your life insurance paid up. Let me find out what happens on Halloween. I don't want the pixies and shifters to have to hide because you have friends over if they have traditions."

Aidoneus shook his head with a smile as he watched the exchange. I doubted he'd ever had a friendly conversation with his father. I'd done some reading on Hades and discovered he was a consummate ladies' man and easy to anger.

"You won't have to worry about falling in because your mom is going to cast an aversion spell around the area. And, it's not an actual hole in the ground. The Hellmouth is very different from the natural entry points to the Underworld. Those are used by everyone to travel through after death."

I should have realized there were regular entrances to the Underworld, but it never dawned on me. "How exactly does that work?"

"When someone dies, their soul travels through the nearest entrance. Regardless if you travel through the Tube in London or Central Station in New York City, every soul arrives at the same place. Cerberus guards the entrance resolutely, and Chiron is there to guide souls to their afterlife. Demons wouldn't dare try to escape through the entrance. They'd end up in my father's dungeon for a decade if they were lucky. It's a one-way street, so to speak."

"So this is a magical ingress and egress into your realm? Why would you want such a thing? Are you taking my mom to the Underworld?" Nina asked.

Aidoneus smiled at Nina. "As it stands, your mom cannot enter the Underworld unless she is dead. Once the Hellmouth is created, that will change. But I promise if she ever comes with me, it will only be for a short trip. I left out the part of how your mom and I will be casting a net between this realm and mine. Then we will anchor it in place with the Hellmouth. Like I said before, it makes sure witches cannot summon higher-level demons. They'd have to do so using the Hellmouth, which will be something most will not ever try."

"Why's that?" I asked.

"Because they will have to open the passage using magic which you and I will feel. I read about Dark magic that can work around the Guardians. Much like the Hellmouth itself, that spell isn't common knowledge. It can only be found in my father's library. It has been thousands of years since anyone managed to break into his palace. I assure you, it is very secure."

"You mentioned explaining more about what is required. I'm not convinced I want Phoebe tying herself and her line to such a construct. It poses a risk to the survival of the Pleiades."

Aidoneus inclined his head to Tarja, where she sat on a tall cushion on her chair. My familiar had been surprisingly silent throughout dinner, allowing us to laugh and talk.

There was no way for me to be upset over her concern. It was valid and something I needed to take into consideration.

"This has never been done before, so I don't have definitive answers." I didn't like those words coming out of Aidon's mouth. "However, I didn't develop the plan based on hope and a prayer. There is plenty of information about the Pleiades' role in balancing magic on Earth. There is also information the Moirai provided. By using an agent of the Underworld, the risk of death lies with them. Phoebe would be sharing the burden of fueling the portal, but if there is an attack on the gateway itself, she will be shielded from harm."

My mom leaned forward and clasped her hands on the table. "How exactly will this work? There isn't land for sale next door, and we aren't moving."

I appreciated my mother's position and agreed. I loved this house. It was no longer empty and eerie. Hattie's last act was to fill it with laughter and love, and I would never betray that legacy. I would ensure it always stayed that way.

Aidoneus took a sip of his iced tea and set the glass down. I could tell he was using the time to collect his thoughts. "The issue of the house is something I plan on speaking to Stella about. I am prepared to do whatever is necessary to procure the right house. If it takes time, then we won't be able to move forward right away. I have to own the land the Hellmouth is on for this to be possible. Once I have that, I will cast blood runes in the best location, followed by wards and an aversion spell beyond that. The last two would be where Phoebe comes in. Once that is done, we will both be required to cast spells and offer a sacrifice to seal the connection."

"Tell me about the sacrifice. Phoebe is not going to give up her ability to have children. She's only forty-three and might want another baby. I know that creates the strongest bond there is, but it is off the table."

37

I wondered at the vehemence in Tarja's tone. I knew Hattie lost her ability to have children after an attack, so I imagined it was a touchy topic for her. "I have no plans to have another child, ever."

"You will not offer your gift of life."

Aidoneus held up a hand. "There's no need to worry about that. I would never ask that of her. I will not be giving it up, either. We can give blood. It isn't Dark magic that I'm talking about, either. Yes, it's Blood magic, but what matters in that is the intent behind your enchantment. The reason for creating the gateway is to protect innocents. There is no greater cause than that. Our intent is pure, and we will not be at risk of being corrupted."

My heart skipped a beat when he said that. I had night-mares about becoming like Myrna. She was a twisted, vile woman that nearly killed me and had my mother and grand-mother held hostage.

Tarja's tail flicked behind her. She was clearly agitated. *"I do not like Blood magic. It is a risky prospect but is a far better option than most others. I recognize the need for her to have a physical bond to the gateway. I will work with you on intent. Phoebe and I will be there to support you every step of the way."*

I swallowed the emotion choking me. "It's my decision, and I would have done it without your consent, Tarja." I needed her and the others to know I was my own witch. Hattie didn't strike me as a follower, and I certainly wasn't. "This is too important to not do. Demons have been hunting in our town for too long. I need you, and the only reason I am going to succeed is because you're in my corner."

"You mentioned a seal. What's that? Is it something I can help do?" I wasn't surprised Nina wanted to be involved. She'd shown interest in magic and being a part of everything from day one.

"The disc will be made of silver and imbued with magic

and carved with runes. I need a professional to manage this task," Aidoneus explained.

Mythia flittered above her Barbie chair. "The pixies can help. We have several master craftsmen in our mound."

"There's also Sebastian in Cottlehill," I pointed out. "Although if there has to be two, they're probably going to have to be the second site."

"You can create the disc, and with Aidoneus's help, you can carve the runes into it."

I gaped at my familiar. "Are you crazy? Do you recall the deformed dragons I gave to my family for protection? I am not a master at manipulating metal. We should get someone else."

"It must be you. By creating the seal, you will be adding another layer of connection. It will make your bond stronger. And, I hope harder to breakthrough."

Aidoneus looked at me with a smile. "Tarja is correct. It will make for a better seal. I would like you to try. If it doesn't work, I can ask Hephaestus."

"I can't possibly create anything stronger than a god!"

Nana glared at me. "Of course, you can. You can do anything you set your mind to."

I wasn't going to get out of this. "Alright. I'll try."

The table exploded in chatter about what it might be like to have a Hellmouth close. My mom mentioned the TV show and asked for reassurance it wouldn't mean we would be inundated.

All I could think about was that Aidoneus wasn't leaving, and I would have to create a disc strong enough to seal a gateway to the Underworld. Just another Tuesday in the Duedonne house.

CHAPTER 5

*M*ythia fluttered through the back door carrying two large baskets. Her wings moved as fast as hummingbirds did, and trying to focus was an exercise in futility. Three more pixies followed her into the house, all carrying their own burdens.

"Set them right here," Mythia directed as she set the baskets in her hand on the large kitchen table. The kitchen had become the place in the house where we spent most of our time. We gathered around the island to talk throughout the day and ate our meals at the table.

"What did you bring us?" Nana asked as she slid off the stool she sat in so often that there were indentations from her butt cheeks on the wood surface. She picked up a piece of silver and tried to bite it.

Mythia cleared her throat. "We have offerings from the clan."

"To help with the seal for the Hellmouth," a pixie woman dressed in a bright purple dress that brought out the rainbow hue in her diaphanous wings. Now that they had set their loads on the table, their wings fluttered at a more sedate pace which meant they were visible.

I waved at the pixies. "I don't believe we've met. I'm Phoebe."

The pixie's cheeks turned pink, and the woman next to her in a pink dress along with the guy in tight breeches and a cream-colored pirate top both looked like they might faint.

Mythia landed on the hand I still had in the air as she pointed to the three. "Phoebe, this is Chlora in the purple, Winnie in the teal, and Thicket. Thicket is our best master craftsman and here to help you with your work."

I lifted Mythia to my shoulder when my arm started aching. While my body was already changing, with more lumps on my thighs than Nana added to her morning coffee, I had a long way to go to get into shape. "Nice to meet you all. I appreciate all the help I can get."

"It's good to see you, Thicket. Been a long time. Have you given more thought to the charm we talked about last time we spoke?"

A smile spread over Thicket's face as he shifted his green gaze to the cat that jumped onto the island next to me. "Tarja. You're looking well. I actually have a charm I made some time ago. Hattie's energy was too weak, but I think perhaps her heir can infuse it with the right enchantment to keep you safe." The tiny pixie reached into a back pocket and pulled out a silver disc that was no bigger than his hand. I couldn't see enough to figure out what was engraved on it.

I gasped when he whispered a word, and the thing grew until it was about an inch in diameter and nearly half his size. "What is that?"

"With the right spell, it's going to be a talisman to protect me when I enter Stuleros. Hattie thought she had a way to protect me, but it seems we need to rethink the approach. After hearing about how much the gods and goddesses meddle, we should bar their interference."

Mythia took off from my shoulder and hovered next to Thicket. I watched as she turned the disc, and I saw an image etched on one side while the other was blank. I assumed it was a rune, but it was nothing like the demonic runes we saw at Myrna's house. They didn't scrape my nerves like the other ones had.

My head snapped in Tarja's direction. "We should add a rune that only allows familiars. I'm not adept at casting, and I don't want to leave your safety to chance. It will cover all options. Is there a way we can leave it in Stuleros to make the pocket dimension, or whatever it is, safe for everyone to visit?"

"That is something we will revisit. Today, we're going to work on the seal. Let's get to it." Tarja jumped off the island and trotted to the door leading to my magic kitchen in the basement.

It was where I made potions and worked with metals and gems. I practiced casting in the attic and trained in the living room while Tsekani built a home gym in half of the attic. The space was big enough to house both areas.

"Stop trying to eat the silver, Nana. Are you and mom coming to watch me make a mess?"

Thicket and the other two pixies stopped and glanced back at me. "Why would you make a mess? You're Hattie's heir."

Nana laughed as she shuffled more than walked. "I wouldn't miss seeing the adoration vanish from their innocent little eyes."

My mother wound an arm through Nana's and helped her. "Stop teasing, mom. Phoebe has learned a lot in the past six months. She rarely starts fires anymore."

The look of horror descended on each of the pixies like an automatic door slamming home. I wasn't going to let their disgust affect me. Going for nonchalant, I shrugged my shoulders and hefted one of the baskets.

Incompetence chased me down like a rabid dog that refused to let me get away when I dropped the basket on my foot. So much for trying to ignore the fact that I wasn't the brilliant witch they believed.

"Shit," I cursed and gripped the basket with both hands. There was no reason to be embarrassed. "I'm not the most skilled. I've only been a witch for six months. If you have a problem with who I am, you can leave. I don't need the negative energy in my house."

Layla clapped me on the shoulder and grabbed two baskets. "You tell 'em, Pheebs. Regardless of your proficiency, you are the heir and owner of the land on which they live. Your magic protects them." My best friend turned to the pixies and glared at them. "Should you need evidence of how powerful she is, test the boundary."

The two tiny women lowered their heads. Chlora blinked her big brown eyes. "I apologize. In the mound, you are a legend. And you carry yourself with such confidence no one could tell you have trouble wielding your magic." I wasn't sure if Chlora's words were a compliment or an insult.

Thicket shook his head from side to side. "Chlora, Winnie, go home. Your help is not needed, and you aren't helping our case any. Daethie will not be happy if you anger Phoebe to the point she forces us to move our mound. My surprise got the better of me. I am honored to help teach you my craft."

"Stop allowing your feelings of inadequacy to take control. Yes, you are a new witch where others expect you to already be one of the best. Your Nana has the right idea of zero fucks to give. Try it on for size and get down here, already."

I laughed at Tarja's two cents and realized I'd spent more time indulging my doubt than I ever had in my life. No wonder I didn't recognize the spiral. "You might be frustrated with me before too long, Thicket. I really don't know much, but I am an excellent student."

I carried the basket I was holding and didn't wait to see if the other pixies left or not. Layla was behind me when Mythia fluttered past us on her way back to the kitchen. "I'll bring the last basket down."

"Thanks," I called after the pixie that had become the smallest member of my new family.

The silver in my hands dropped with a thud on the empty table in the room. Shelves lined most of one wall in the room, and there were some cabinets next to them. Both contained ingredients for spells. Herbs, crystals, oils, candles with precious metals, and gems are located in the drawers.

I hadn't realized it before, but there was a pleasant hum coming from the silver that told me it came from the heart of the mound where the earth magic of their kind pooled. That energy seeped into everything around them and spread throughout my property. The stones and metal removed from the core of the mound were powerful on their own.

I grabbed the nuggets from the basket and set them on the wood table. "How much will we need?"

Thicket set his container next to mine. "We will need all of it."

"Maybe even more. It needs to be three feet in diameter and at least a foot thick so we can settle it securely in the ground."

"That's big. Do we have enough?" I dumped the rest of my nuggets on the pile.

Layla turned one basket over, then the other, adding hers to the mix. "There are five more baskets, so I'd bet there will be plenty."

"If not, we can use the supply you have here."

I glanced at Tarja and shook my head. "I don't have much. Just one drawer."

44

Mythia snorted then. "You have more than you've seen. Hattie had a vault hidden in the garage. It's yours now."

Of course, she did. I shook my head, unable to comprehend the enormity of what I had inherited. I was just glad it helped the entire coven. It made me feel better about suddenly having so much money.

"Okay, so we have enough. I say we start with this pile, then assess. What do I need to do now?"

Thicket took a basket from Mythia and dumped it to the table. The wood table groaned from the weight, making me worry it was too much and would break. The last thing I needed was the platform breaking while I was working with the silver.

I focused on reinforcing and supporting the middle of the table. I added steel girders in my mind, so the entire length had posts beneath it. "Et evidentior firmamentum."

"Good thinking. The table is a thousand years old, and there is more weight than I anticipated. Your instincts are coming along nicely."

Thicket landed on the edge of the silver closest to me. "We need to start by melting the segments together to form one block before trying to shape it."

I nodded my head and called my fire. Purple flames danced over my hands, and I enjoyed the rush I felt when I released my magic. It invigorated and energized me. I threw it out in front of me like a blanket and draped it over the silver.

The metal sizzled, and an acrid odor filled the room along with smoke. Thicket flew into the air, waving his hands frantically. "No! No fire. You're burning the energy in the silver."

I gasped and cut my fire off immediately. The room smelled awful, and the smoke was so thick it choked me. I bent over when a coughing fit overtook me. Coughing echoed from every corner of the room, creating a chorus that belonged in the ICU.

"Told you." Nana's voice cracked and broke into hacking.

Before I could manage to chant a spell to dispel the smoke, wind blew through the room. It carried the stench away and left the sweet smell of flowers. Mythia hovered above the silver with both arms out.

"Thanks, Thia." I tilted my head, and my upper lip curled. The silver on top was blackened with soot. "Well, I made a mess. Guess I'd better clean it up."

"Do not use a blanket cleanse spell, or you will strip the energy inside, and we need it."

"Thanks for the heads up. Next time, start your explanation with no fire, Thicket. To us mundies, flames are the best way to melt objects."

"Noted." He brushed soot from his clothes while I focused on washing the dark stains only from the silver. *"Deluo."*

The soot fell from the nuggets that were now slightly melted. They dropped to the table before another wind gathered it into a mini-black funnel. Layla opened the small rectangular window, and the tornado blew outside.

I brushed my hands together and turned back to the table. Thicket landed on a bare corner of the table. "Now, you need to call on the earth element, so you can bond to the metal. Then we will be manipulating the cellular structure to shape it as we want."

He might as well be trying to walk me through brain surgery. The steps seemed impossible. Thankfully, I'd worked at a teaching hospital and had listened to surgeons giving residents step-by-step instructions on how to do complex and delicate procedures, like heart transplants and clipping aneurysms.

"Face the north, take off your shoes, so your feet touch the stone

floor, and call on the earth element out loud before using a malleable spell."

I turned in a circle before Thicket grabbed my hand and tugged. "This is north."

"Thanks." I toed off one shoe, then the other, and pulled off my socks. I needed to soften the silver so I could shape it. "*Mollit.*"

The second the spell left my lips, the silver started morphing and sagging until the nuggets blended into one mushy pile. The pile started spreading out and came close to running over the edges of the table.

Thicket cried out and chanted a spell that stopped the metal from drooping over the sides. "Hellooo," Stella called out from the top of the stairs.

I smiled, grateful for the reprieve. "Down here."

Stella's black heels preceded her, followed by dark blue trousers. Finally, her beautiful smile and perfect blonde hair arrived as she stepped off the last stair. "What are we up to now?"

"I'm making a seal for a Hellmouth."

Her face scrunched up, and she pursed her lips. "That is a powerful seal that will keep demons locked in the Underworld?"

"You spoke with Aidon, I see."

She nodded her head. "I did. We paid a visit to the neighbors this morning to offer them double what their house and land are worth. They had no plans of moving and are thinking it over."

My heart raced when I thought about Aidon moving in next door. After Miles, I never wanted to tangle my life with a guy again. Having him, next door seemed like the best solution.

And, while I know he was moving so close for purposes of the Hellmouth, I couldn't deny I hoped a tiny part of him did it because he wanted more with me, too. I'd even dreamed he came up with the idea so he could intertwine our lives. Wishful thinking, I know.

"Do you think they'll sell?"

Stella shrugged her shoulders. "I can usually get a read on things like this, but I'm not sure yet."

"Greed will make them sell eventually," Nana interjected.

"I agree," my mom said. "If it was me, I would wait a bit to see if I could get more from the guy. Anyone who offers double really wants the house and is likely to pay more."

I hated to say it, but they were probably right. I wanted to believe mundies were above being greedy and trying to manipulate a situation to get more money, but I knew better.

Stella poked the silver, and her finger left an indentation. "I was thinking the same thing. Although, if that's the case, they hid their desire for more very well."

"If this is going to happen, I'd better get back to it. We will need this to open the Hellmouth."

"*Or you could take a break from that and try to astral project to Stuleros. When you mentioned adding a rune to Thicket's charm, I've wanted to see if you can enter in your astral form.*"

Stella's head swiveled like a wiper on a windshield. "Thicket?"

Thicket flew in front of her and hovered. "That would be me. I'm the silversmith in the mound and came to help Phoebe with the seal."

Stella smiled. "You're a brave man. I hope you're getting hazard pay."

I rolled my eyes at my friend and nearly laughed at Thicket's confused expression. Instead, I refocused on Tarja's suggestion. "If I can astral project, I might be able to cast a spell binding the amulet to the pocket dimension."

"*My thinking exactly. You need to remove all thoughts from your mind and focus only on my energy and your connection to*

48

me. It'll help if you sit down when doing this. Once out of your body, it will collapse."

My mom stood up from one of the two armchairs and gestured for me to take it. Usually, I would never take a seat from my mother, but I had no desire to get a concussion while trying this.

I sat down and took several deep breaths shoving thoughts of the seal, Aidoneus and my family watching me out of my mind. It wasn't easy, but once my gaze was unfocused, I was able to think about the cozy sensation I associated with Tarja. And the chain I envisioned as our connection.

Keeping only those thoughts in mind, I closed my eyes. *"Supercresco."*

At first, there didn't seem to be any changes. The buzz of familiar energy remained around me. Between one breath and the next, I lost the ability to feel my body. My eyes snapped open, and I was floating in a white mist.

There was power all around. It didn't sting me like Dark energy but didn't welcome me, either. I kept my mind focused on Tarja while telling my feet to move forward. It wasn't until I felt her to my left that I was able to take a step.

The fog coalesced around me like a cocoon. I didn't let that stop me. Keeping my steps firm, I continued until the mist disappeared, and I found myself in a meadow the size of two football fields. Flowers covered the ground, making the air sweet. Trees were surrounding the grassy area.

Without having to touch a trunk, I knew they acted as the border to this dimension. Tarja bounded through the trees and splashed through a creek I hadn't noticed before.

"It worked. There has never been a witch in Stuleros. We might be able to move forward with a plan to repopulate the familiars, after all."

I spun in a slow circle. "This place seems safe. Why can't you start now?"

A cold wind blew against my back, making the peaceful atmosphere vanish along with the sweet scent. When I turned, my breath caught in my throat. Figures floated at the far edge of the meadow, but I couldn't exactly call them ghosts. They weren't humanoid at all. The head was evident on each distorted, grey body, and the red eyes radiated violence.

"Tarja, get out!" Instinct screamed at me that this was the Tainted at work.

My mind started working through the problem at a million miles a minute. I'd bet the corrupted witches had a connection to the realm through the familiars they'd killed before. If that was the case, they wouldn't hesitate to kill Tarja and take her power.

"I don't know if they can injure your astral body, but you need to leave, too."

"I'll be right behind you. I want you gone first."

Tarja didn't respond, but I suddenly couldn't feel her. I had no idea how to get back to my body. I freaked out for a split second before reversing her instructions. This time I thought of my body. Every stretch mark, scar, and roll.

The floating sensation vanished, and I jumped from the chair the second I felt the jeans pinching the bulge of my belly. "Tarja!"

"I'm here. We did it. This might be possible."

I smiled at the excitement in her mental voice. It practically vibrated from her. I'd never heard or felt her so happy before. I would do everything in my power to make sure she and the familiars regained Stuleros as their domain.

CHAPTER 6

"*H*old still," Nina warned me for the tenth time since I sat down at the vanity in my room.

It was Halloween, and she wanted all of us to dress up as witches. Stella and Nana jumped at the idea. My mom and I groaned and complained before capitulating. There were only so many more moments in life where I would be able to bond like this with my daughter.

"Are you almost done?"

"Yep. I just need to finish the eye shadow."

"Wow! You look great, Pheebs." I opened the eye Nina wasn't working on and saw my best friend standing in the doorway.

Stella's blonde hair was in two braids, and her make-up was perfect, as usual. She had on pink striped stockings, low-heeled, lace-up boots, and a fluffy black skirt in place of her business attire. Her top was fitted to her torso where mine was loose. It was the pointy hat on top of her head that finished the costume.

"Alright. All done."

Nina moved away from the mirror, and my mouth

dropped open when I caught my reflection. She'd given me smokey, sexy eyes and rosy cheeks. My lips shimmered with glitter, and my brown hair was curled above my shoulders. The black hat hid the top of my head and, to my surprise, didn't make me look ridiculous.

Hats didn't look good on me. I didn't have the face or youth for it. Seemed like there was an exception to that rule. I smiled and stood up to embrace my daughter. "I love it. Thank you."

What she selected for me was perfect. My costumes had a longer skirt and loose top where hers had a shorter skirt and bustier. And it looked outstanding on her.

I couldn't see me shoving my rolls into the clothes, let alone my ninety-year-old grandmother. "Are Nana and Gammy downstairs?"

"They're in the kitchen," Stella told me.

The doorbell echoed throughout the house, and Nina dashed through the door. "I've got it." She was excited to hand out candy. I told her not to expect many visitors. We lived in a pretty remote area. Seems I was wrong about that.

My feet froze on the landing when I saw Aidoneus standing in the entryway to my house. Stella tugged my arm and practically drug me the rest of the way. "Aidon. Did you come to hang out with us this evening?"

We stopped in front of him, and we were both speechless for a second. He recovered first. "I wanted to check in and let you know I didn't sense any demons, aside from Marilee in town, so if Nina wanted to go out with her friends, it is safe."

He was dressed in his usual black jeans and leather jacket over a dark Henley. And just as sexy as ever. "Trying to earn brownie points with the surly teenager?"

Nina growled, "Mom." We both ignored her. She'd been angry when I told her she couldn't go out to a party with her friends tonight.

Nana and my mom entered from the left and joined us. "Why did we have to dress up if he isn't?" Nana complained.

Aidoneus laughed. "Halloween isn't really my favorite night. Too many demons try to escape and join the chaos on Earth. You all look wonderful." His eyes shifted to me and stayed there when he spoke.

"It's not too much?"

He shook his head, and his sapphire eyes glowed with desire. "It's classy and sexy and a reflection of your powers. Even you, Nana. You, too, Mollie. You might not be able to cast spells or conjure fire, but Phoebe is a witch in part because of you both and the power she inherited through you two."

Nana preened and smiled. "You're a brilliant man. The first one in this house that's noticed where some of it comes from. I'll give credit to Hattie, she made Phoebe magical, but she already had some power."

"I suspect you have a witch somewhere in your family line. Phoebe's innate power was one reason Hattie selected her. The other was her pure heart."

"I thought it was because of the amulet Sebastian made for me," I recalled her saying something about it.

The scratchy hacking that represented Tarja's laughter filled my head. *"She thought you were aware of the hidden world of supernaturals. The enchantment had a strong charm on it. She was surprised every time you asked about Tsekani or mentioned Evanora. Despite your obvious ignorance, she started the process of passing everything to you. She said she knew the second she met you."*

Tears threatened and had me blinking furiously to keep them at bay. I didn't want to ruin Nina's hard work. "I thought she was batty when she'd tell me stuff like the ghost was trying to get my attention and a dragon lived on her property. I even considered calling about getting new scans to make sure she didn't have mets in her brain or the onset of dementia." I leaned more toward old age, causing an issue than the spread of her cancer, but both had been possibilities in my mind.

"Hattie was a batty old broad. And, I clearly didn't know her well enough. I suspect she and I were cheated out of many fun nights," Nana observed.

"Hattie closed down after the attack that almost took her life and left her barren. It was my job to push her more, but I gave her room to heal. I knew the grief she went through over losing the ability to have kids."

I'd been blessed with two beautiful kids. It was for them that I would marry Miles all over again. I couldn't imagine being told I could never have them. It would break my heart.

"After getting to know you, I can honestly say the two of you would have been friends. There weren't many women her age that appreciated her candor." Tarja's comment to Nana surprised me. I imagined Hattie would have loved Nana.

The doorbell interrupted the conversation as Nina bounced to the door with a Lambeau-Field-stadium-sized bowl of candy. Her shoulders dropped as she turned her body. "Oh, it's you."

For the second time that night, my jaw hit my chest. What was it with the surprises? I had no desire to talk business or coven with Lilith tonight. I'd give her a quick brush off and go back to ogling Aidoneus. Perhaps we'd find a corner to make out.

I started forward. "Lilith. To what do I owe the pleasure?"

"She's off the clock," Nana called.

Lilith's thin lips were pinched, and her hazel eyes were narrowed. "Are you mocking what you've become? As you know, we don't wear witch hats or those infernal striped socks."

"I see you passed the line when they were giving out the ability to have fun," I replied. "Why are you here?"

Lilith took a breath and let it out slowly. She was likely counting to five in her head. Wonder if it worked for her. "You're coming with me to the All Hallows Eve celebration at Nightshadow Grove."

I clenched my hands into fists. "And here I thought you'd come to tell me our stock was up by fifty percent. I didn't prearrange to have Dr. Nichols here tonight. You're going to have to come back."

My mom and Nana laughed while everyone else looked from me to Lilith. The quip was lost on her because she didn't know the mundie doctor.

Lilith crossed the threshold and paused just inside the door. "You are the leader of the coven. We can't have the celebration without you. If you bothered to have one conversation with me about your role, you'd know this. It's cruel to refuse to go and deny the entire coven the opportunity to come together and celebrate. This night is about far more than what you might think of as a silly party. When the members dance under the moon together on one of the sacred nights, it bestows power on each member and rejuvenates them."

The woman was excellent with the guilt trip. She had me wanting to apologize profusely when I hadn't known about it before now. "Sounds like we're going to a party."

"I'll stay here with Mollie and Amelia. You, Stella, and Nina have fun."

My familiar was the freaking best. I was going to drag them all, and she'd let me know without making a spectacle of it that only witches should attend. "Thank you. Do you want to ride with Nina and me, Stella?"

Stella had a smile a mile wide on her face. "I'll drive. I remember the way."

Nina was already hugging my mom and Nana before I could tell them goodbye. Aidoneus walked us to the driveway and pulled me into a brief but intense kiss before releasing me and walking to his car.

I stumbled to Stella's car, glad she was behind the wheel. My mind was spinning after that.

* * *

THE MAIN ROAD leading to Nightshadow Grove was as dark as I recalled. Unlike last time the turnoff was easy to see given the wrought iron lanterns illuminated on each side.

Nina grabbed the sides of my seat as she sat behind me. "Those look like the lampposts you want to get, mom."

"Yes, they do. I'll have to ask if there is a local craftsman." There were three tapered iron holders with glass protecting the flame on each side and ornate metalwork along each roof. The posts were ten feet tall and looked like they'd been fixed into the ground. How had we missed them last time?

The dirt road leading to the house had trees lining both sides. They still blocked the moonlight, but the oppressive darkness was alleviated by the lanterns hung on hooks every few feet. Sparkly black garland wound around the poles. These would have been nice to have last time.

Stella pulled inline in the busy circular drive. There was an attendant taking cars as people climbed out. The front of the two-story Victorian house and wrap-around porch were all lit with the same lanterns. There weren't other decorations around the outside. I wondered if there were any inside.

Nina shoved an arm through the seats. "Look at those gingerbread accents. I'd pick different colors, but I love this house." I looked at the light green siding and blue-grey, pink and yellow accents. I had to agree with her. Maybe I'd let her pick the colors next time it had to be painted.

"I want the rectangular room up there. I love the copper roof on the ceiling and the way it sits above the house."

Nina laughed. "That's because it looks like a lighthouse, mom." She knew me so well.

I was laughing when Stella stopped in front of the valet a second later. We got out and grabbed our hats, shoving them on our heads. I had insisted on wearing them, saying the coven needed to know we had a sense of humor. Stella gave a wide-eyed teenager her keys before we climbed the stairs to the porch.

The valet wore a black cape over dark clothing. The witches walking up the path to the house were all wearing dark blue robes embroidered with silver stars along the hem and lapel. A woman I didn't know glanced over her shoulder, lifting the material to hide her expression. I saw the disdain at the same time I noticed the cloth was thick and likely heavy.

The front door was open, but everyone was heading around the porch to the backyard. Nina poked her head inside. "There isn't much in here. Just a big table. Did they tear down walls?"

"I think so," Stella told her. "They need an interior decorator in here to give the place some character."

I tugged Nina's arm and turned her to follow those in front of us. We were definitely garnering attention because the witches in front kept looking over their shoulders. When I looked back, there was more whispering and pointing at us.

I quickened my pace and lifted my chin. "You don't like the *pilleus cornutus*? Not that we're going for the horned look, per se."

The silence was suddenly deafening. The entire coven stopped talking and was looking at us. Lilith stepped forward. "Lady Phoebe decided to dress up for the holiday. She isn't insulting our kind; she's fully embracing what she has become, and because she grew up a mundie, this is what it looks like for her."

I inclined my head, appreciating Lilith backing me up. Conversation resumed, and I leaned toward Stella. "Have you noticed the only guys here are the valets? Are all witches female?"

Lilith rolled her eyes at me. "Yes. Men can be warlocks, and if they can wield any of the elements, they are mages. Our coven is all female."

"There are more than thirteen members," Nina pointed out. Looking around the yard, there had to be thirty, maybe more. "I read in our grimoire there is power in that number, and it was best to keep coven numbers at thirteen."

Lilith smiled at my daughter, clearly happy with her knowledge. "The number thirteen is significant for witches and covens. With the Pleiades located in Camden, our numbers have always been twenty times higher than any other. Hattie and her predecessors refused to deny membership. It would have created unnecessary tension among the community if they weren't allowed in. Hence, they created the council, which we limit to thirteen members. We're about ready to start. You two wait right here."

Stella binclined her head and remained at Nina's side while I followed Lilith to the table in the center of the room. The weight of everyone's eyes made me shift in the low-heeled, lace-up boots I was wearing.

Needing a distraction, I looked around. Lanterns were the only decoration visible anywhere. The backyard had a large flagstone patio with two long tables laden with food and drinks. In addition, there was a smaller table in the middle of the yard, plus a bonfire raging twenty feet from the house, well away from the surrounding forest. The flames were at least four feet tall.

Lilith gestured for Bridget to come forward. Bridget held a tray with several items on it, including what looked like a loaf of bread, as she approached us at the empty table in the middle of the grass. What the hell did a loaf of bread have to do with anything?

Bridget held the tray out, and Lilith grabbed a jar. "This is powdered incense. We pour it in the shape of a pentagram on the table to let go of old sorrows, anger, and anything not befitting new beginnings."

Lilith dumped the incense in a perfect pentagram that I could never replicate. I needed her to do this every year. When she was done, she put the jar back and grabbed three candles. "These represent the triple goddess. Mother, maiden, and crone. We light them in her honor."

Lilith handed me the lighter, and I lit the candles while she spoke. "In honor of the triple goddess on this sacred night of Samhain. All the ancient ones, from time before time. To those behind the veil."

She paused and rapped the altar three times, then took the lighter from me and lit the incense. When she was done with that, she recited a blessing. "For this bread, wine, and salt, we ask the blessings of mother, maiden, and crone. And the gods who guard the gate of the world." The smell of incense replaced the earthy smell of the forest around the property.

Lilith turned to Bridget and picked up a jar of what looked like salt. I thought she would add it to the pentagram, but she sprinkled it over the loaf of bread on the tray, then tore off a chunk and handed it to me. I popped it in my mouth. That seemed to spur activity.

Clio stepped forward and tore chunks off, handing them out as coven members came forward. Stella and Nina were in the line. Of course, my daughter flashed me a big smile before moving to the side. I loved how excited she was by a magical life since it was thrust upon her as much as it was me. Lilith handed me a much-needed glass of wine.

When I searched for my daughter and Stella, I saw them both holding a glass, as well. My daughter was only sixteen, and I took a step to take it from her then stopped. This was part of the celebration. I would allow her a sip.

Following my gut, I lifted my glass into the air. "To the Goddess Hecate. Thank you for the bountiful blessings you've given us." Energy rose from the ground and descended from the sky. For a second, I thought it would smash us, but it dissipated and saturated the area.

That was some kind of signal because everyone headed for the food, talking and laughing. My connection to the coven got stronger as I visited and got to know them. Before I knew it, the cloaks were removed, and the women were dancing around the bonfire.

I looked at Stella and Nina and shrugged shoulders. "When in Rome!"

Nina giggled and raced for the fire with a young woman she seemed to hit it off with. Stella grabbed my hand, and we joined the fun. I never imaged I would feel connected to these women. I hadn't really given them much of my time or energy. I was going to have to change that.

CHAPTER 7

Sweat dripped into my eye, making it burn. I paused, trying to coax the silver molecules into a man-hole cover on steroids. As a registered nurse, I understood cellular make-up. I was able to visualize what I thought was the basis for silver, but I didn't speak metal.

I never was any good at sweet-talking others. Sarcasm and laying it all out were my love languages. My eye started twitching, and my mind wandered to how I fought the urge to throttle Clio every time we had a business meeting together. In my opinion the coroner had no business in these gatherings anyway, but I also didn't care to ask Lilith why she was there when she showed up.

My focus was usually on the fact that there was no reason to tell me how this person or that one was recently involved in a car accident and missed a couple days of work to get their car fixed. Their kid got sick, then their mom fell and broke her hip as a way to explain why a quarterly report wasn't done.

It didn't matter to me. They didn't get the report done, and no one else stepped up to help. The rest didn't matter. I wasn't firing anyone, but I really didn't need ten minutes of excuses. I needed a plan of action to get the reports done, so the shareholders and board members didn't get upset and start calling me.

I wasn't a businesswoman and had no desire to field those calls. I had too much magical crap to deal with, like the silver seal for the Hellmouth. I looked up at Thicket. "How do you make this look so easy? I can't get it to spread out in a circle."

Thicket paused where he was flying over the disc, examining my work. "You're overthinking your approach."

I threw my hands up in the air. "How is that possible? I keep sending the image I want at the metal, and it doesn't work."

Nana snored softly from the armchair in the corner. My mom was reading in the other one with Selene sitting near the bookshelves a couple of feet away. Mom set her book down and looked up at us. "You're making progress, sweetheart. Just keep trying."

I was going to try something different this time. I was a tactile learner, which was why I excelled during the practical part of nursing school. Calling up what I wanted to do with the silver, I held my hands over as much of the metal as I could reach. "*Plaque figura.*"

My palms heated as I pressed them to the surface and pushed them out in circles. The silver softened and moved with my palms. It wasn't what Thicket had suggested, but I felt movement, so I continued.

Footsteps echoed down the stairs, making my head swivel. I kept my focus on what I was doing until my son's smile dropped from his face. Jean-Marc stood there agog. His jaw was slack, and his eyes, the exact blue of Nana's, were wide with fear.

I jerked my hands up and winced when I saw the red

palm prints I left on the silver. "Hey, buddy. It's so good to see you. What brings you home before Thanksgiving?"

We weren't expecting him back so soon. He was in his second year in college and moved into his own apartment, so he didn't come home as often as when we lived closer and was in the dorm.

My mom jumped to her feet and embraced him in a hug. The commotion woke Nana, and she tried to get up, as well. Selene was to her and helping her up before I ever reached her side. My stomach roiled. Was he going to accept me now that I had magic?

We'd hidden it from him last time he visited. Seeing his expression right now, I knew I made the right decision. When it was evident that he wasn't going to reply, Nina stepped in for him. "He has the weekend free and wanted to come home. If you ask me, he misses Gammy's home-cooked meals."

My mom preened and smiled. Jean-Marc had given her the nickname Gammy when he couldn't say, grandma. "Let's go get you something to eat."

Jean-Marc shook his head. "What's going on here? How were you touching that hot silver, and what is that?" He pointed to the pixie hovering over the lump.

A rock settled in my gut. How was I going to explain Thicket? There was no explaining away the tiny man with iridescent wings and breeches. His red hair and wide green eyes couldn't pass as plastic. As if Jean-Marc would believe he was looking at a flying doll.

Nana patted Jean-Marc's cheek. It was awkward as she stood on tiptoe to reach him. He was over six feet tall where she was around five-foot-two. "That's Thicket. He's a pixie. We have some news to share with you, but you're going to need to sit down for this. And, I want some of that tart from Marilee's bakery."

"You should eat lunch first, mom." My mom was the first to head up. Selene didn't want any part of the conversation and was hot on her heels.

Nina ascended with Nana, who scowled at her daughter's back. "I've earned the right to eat dessert for lunch if I want."

Jean-Marc didn't seem to hear their conversation as he stood staring at Thicket, who remained in the same spot. I wrapped an arm around his waist. "You alright?"

Jean-Marc must have heard the wobble in my voice because his eyes were soft and loving when he looked at me. He was my affectionate little man and always had been since the day he was born.

His arms wound around me. "I'm honestly not sure, but I'm glad I'm here."

A weight lifted from my chest, and I hugged him back. "Let's get up there before Nana eats all the tart. You've got to try some."

"Sounds good to me." He looked over at Thicket as we started up.

When we reached the third stair, I paused. "Are you coming, Thicket? You should be there, too. You can help me find the right tools for our next step." He'd asked what I would use to engrave the runes, and I realized I had nothing. His supplies were like toothpicks and of no use to me.

The pixie's gaze went from mine to Jean-Marc's before he nodded. "If you're sure. I don't want to frighten your son."

"I'm not afraid of you. You're not even six inches tall." I recognized the bravado in my son's voice and pushed him to keep moving. The last thing I needed was for him to piss off Thicket and discover how strong his kind actually was. Besides, I wanted my son to get along and like my new friends. I considered them family.

"I'll have you know size isn't everything," Thicket said as he zipped past us and through the door.

I couldn't help but burst into laughter. The defensive way he said that reminded me of the countless times I'd heard guys argue that size didn't matter. Jean-Marc joined my laughter, and the tight band around my chest eased a fraction. It was going to be alright. It would take time, but in the end, it was going to work out.

"What's so funny?" Nina asked as we entered.

"They're laughing about a guy's size not mattering," Layla said with a chuckle. She was sitting on the stool next to Nana. "Hey, Jean-Marc. Good to see you again."

His gaze shot to Thicket and widened when he noticed Mythia next to him. I grabbed his hand and practically shoved him onto the last stool. "What Gammy was referring to earlier is the fact that I'm a witch now." I paused, letting that sink in.

His forehead scrunched up. "What? How is that possible? How come I never knew? Is that why dad had an affair?"

My pulse jumped, and my jaw clenched. It wasn't Jean-Marc accusing me. I knew my son. He was trying to make sense of his world. "No. That isn't why. I cannot tell you why your father did what he did. I didn't become a witch until I moved back home." I briefly told him how I was attacked by Myrna, and to save my life, Hattie had given me her magic, thus making me a Pleiades.

He rubbed a hand down his face. "I had no idea witches were real. And faeries. Wow. But it makes sense."

Mythia landed on the counter at the same time Tarja jumped on the counter. "We're pixies, a type of Fae. We're from Eidothea, the Fae realm, but other creatures originate in your world."

Jean-Marc reached out to pet my familiar while he watched the tiny woman. "What do you mean, there's more?"

"There are shifters, vampires, ghouls, and demons, to name a

few. And magical cats that are a witch's familiars and can speak telepathically."

Jean-Marc snatched his hand back and jumped off the stool. He stumbled over the chair and started falling backward. I lunged for him, but Layla caught him before he got hurt.

She steadied him and let go. He was shaking as he looked around the room. I went to him and wrapped an arm around his shoulders. "It's okay. I'm sorry I kept this from you. It wasn't something I wanted to tell you over the phone then when you visited for your birthday. I didn't want to ruin your day."

He was pale, but he sat down again and stroked Tarja again. "You're a magical cat?"

Tarja met his gaze. "*Yes. I'm your mother's familiar. I help her with her magic, and I will help your sister when her time comes.*"

Jean-Marc's eyes went wide. "Will I get a familiar?"

I smiled at him and shook my head from side to side. "No, son. I'm sorry. Witchcraft is a woman thing. If I had you now, you would be a warlock or a mage depending on your abilities, but the magic didn't go to you when it was given to me."

He cocked his head to the side. "That's not true. I have magic."

My jaw dropped, and I looked at Tarja, who stood right in front of my son and scanned him. "*Explain what you mean by that.*"

Jean-Marc glanced around at everyone, lifted his hand, then dropped it when Tsekani came in the back door.

Tseki threw up his hands and paused. "Woah. What did I interrupt? The tension in here is thick."

"My son was about to show us his magic," I told the dragon shifter.

Tsekani's green eyes, which were an exotic color for his Asian heritage, went wide. "He knows?"

I inclined my head. "He saw me working on the Hell-mouth cover."

Jean-Marc's head swung in my direction. "What?"

I sighed. Crap, I needed to watch what I was saying. I wanted to find out what he was talking about. "That's a story for later. First, I want to find out what magic you have."

Thicket landed next to Mythia, who stood next to Tarja. Nina stood next to me, and Nana sat next to Marc with Layla on her other side. We all watched and waited to see what he would do. He focused his gaze on the glass in front of Nana.

She cried out when it moved across the island and to my son's outstretched hand. He smiled up at me, and I couldn't miss the relief in his expression when his gaze met mine.

I'd been so caught up in my world that I hadn't asked more about the stress I could hear in his voice when we spoke and when he visited. At the time, I'd assumed it was because he was in college, and it's a stressful time with assignments and tests.

"That's so cool. Even I can't do that. Why can't I do that?" I directed the last part to my familiar.

"You can, but it's not the same as what he did. Mages call on the elements and use their powers in their spells, but they cannot manipulate the elements. Witches have many powers that can be confusing, like your witch fire. Most would say that's elemental magic, but it's not. It is a part of you, not an element in nature, which is why it's purple in color. Mages can manipulate the elements without the use of chants."

Jean-Marc ran a hand through his hair. "Is everyone here a witch? Do you have power, too, Gammy? What about you, Nana?"

Nana had a pout of her face that drew the sides of her mouth down. The wrinkles around her mouth deepened with the move. "We didn't get crap. How is that fair? I'd make a great witch. That one is a wolf shifter, that one is a dragon, and that one is a ghoul. You already know the pixies are Fae."

Jean-Marc turned and faced Tsekani, who had remained next to the back doors. Apparently, a wolf shifter and ghoul didn't spark his interest like a dragon. "You turn into a dragon?"

"Told you he'd love that," I muttered.

Tsekani laughed. "I am a Loong dragon. I was made by a witch, unlike most shifters who are Born this way."

"I was made a wolf, as well. By the same witch, actually. We're the only made we know of and not accepted by born shifters," Layla added.

Tsekani nodded and crossed to the fridge, where he grabbed a soda. "Which is why we asked Hattie for asylum."

Selene stepped forward. I could see how nervous she was. "And, I'm a ghoul that came to your mom for help. Someone did this to me against my will, and she's helping me."

Jean-Marc started at Selene for several silent seconds before he sighed and shook his head. "Your life has been downright crazy. I can't believe I've been stressed about making shit move with my mind when you've had to face all this, plus something about a Hellmouth, which makes me think of that show with the vampire slayer. I thought I was losing my mind. I can only imagine what this has been like for you."

"You have every reason to be freaked out. That isn't something that happens to normal people," I told my son. "Did anyone see you do this? And, why didn't you mention something sooner?"

"That's why I came home. I'm here to tell you something is wrong with me. It didn't happen until after I stayed here during the summer. At least now I get why you guys were so secretive back then. I assumed you were dating that guy with messy black hair and didn't want me to know."

I gaped at Jean-Marc and felt my cheeks heat. Nina, however, laughed. "That guy is the son of Hades, bro. And mom is dating him! She's creating the Hellmouth with his help."

Jean-Marc was off his chair again. "Mother! You're dating the son of the devil?"

Nana grabbed his pants and pulled him down. "Stop chastising her as if she is doing something wrong. She deserves to have a hot guy that loves her after your father."

My mom patted his shoulder. "Besides, Hades isn't the devil. That's a different mythology. Hades is the God of the Underworld, which isn't Hell like you think of it. Think Elysian Fields, Tartarus, and Cerberus. Now, let's talk about why your powers manifested after you stayed here."

"He shouldn't have inherited any power in the exchange. Hattie and I researched for weeks before she gave you the power. Everything that we discovered indicated only your daughter would get the magic because it is passed down through the female line."

"Which is why we should have gotten some of the power," Nana grumbled.

I shrugged my shoulders. "I agree, Nana. So, if he shouldn't have it, why did he manifest it?"

Tarja tilted her head. *"You visited Mt. Battie this summer, right?"*

Nina, Jean-Marc, and I all nodded our heads. "Yeah, I took them because I wanted to share the area with them. I thought they'd like the hike and love the view."

"There are powerful ley lines in the area that likely kick-started his powers. You will need to be careful, Jean-Marc. Regardless of why or how you received your magic, you now have it and need to read and learn what you can. I'll send some books with you, but one thing you need to keep in mind is that warlocks need to remain near ley lines. Or visit a powerful area often to recharge your

energy. Otherwise, you run the risk of giving in to the desire to steal it from others."

My gut twisted in a knot, and I felt like I was going to be sick. What had I gotten my kids into? I never wanted their lives to be so complicated. When I looked at them, they were all smiles, and Nina seemed excited that her brother had magic, too.

Nana snapped her fingers. "Tseki, you're going to take Mollie and me up to that mountain and carry me to the spot where these lines converge."

I cocked my head, glad for the reprieve from the guilt of a moment before. "Why do you want to go there, Nana?" I had a suspicion, but I wanted to hear her say it.

"So, we can get our powers." Nana's tone screamed, duh. "These old bones just need a little jolt, is all. Our family is special. That's why things haven't been the way they expected."

"That could work, right, Tarja?" My mom sounded just as excited by the idea. There was no way I was going to stop them from trying to kick start their powers. There was no harm in them trying. Nothing was going to come of it, anyway.

At that moment, I was going to hug my son and look into ley lines in North Carolina and develop a plan to make sure he doesn't Turn. The Hellmouth seal could wait. This was more important right now.

CHAPTER 8

lipping on my blinker, I almost pulled into the parking spot before I slammed on the brakes. Some guy driving his midlife crisis around, sped into it before I could. I laid on the horn as if it had the answers to the universe. "Asshole!"

Jean-Marc asked for Gammy's stew before returning home tomorrow, which was why I was at Hannaford being cut off by a guy with a dead rat on top of his head. Channeling my peaceful mother, I drove to the next spot and parked the car.

I grabbed my purse and jumped out of the car. The weather was getting chilly, and I grabbed my sweater before locking the door. Armed with my marching orders and my purse, I crossed the parking lot.

"Lady Phoebe! What are you doing here?" Clio was waving as she bent over the handle of her cart like she was preparing to run a race while pushing groceries. Her skinny feet slacking on the pavement as she rushed.

I caught the grimace and now channeled my inner stepford wife. "It's just Phoebe. I'm getting some groceries...at the grocery store." What did she think I was doing? Summoning demons?

The healer stopped next to me with a chuckle. I had no idea how she moved so fast in those death stilts and that tight dress. The red fabric hugged her body like a glove. She looked great, but the clothes looked uncomfortable as hell.

"Of course, that was a stupid question. I get nervous around you, and I have no idea why." Perhaps because every coroner I'd ever met at the hospital was incredibly socially awkward. They worked with the dead all day. Not a lot of time to hone social skills.

I cleared my throat and tugged an empty cart from the stall where they were lined up like soldiers ready for duty. I needed the shield between us. Hearing I made her nervous gave me a complex. There was no reason for her to be worried. I was a baby at magic compared to her.

"My ex-husband is the only one that should be nervous in my proximity. I can see you're busy. No, wait a minute. Do you know anything about mages?" I needed to use every resource available to me. I trusted Tarja with my life, but I wanted to put Clio at ease and see if she had any other information. You never knew.

She clicked her tongue, and her focus faded, reminding me of a computer that was accessing files. "I know they're men that can do elemental magic rather than using the elements to fuel their spells. They need regular infusions of energy, but then all men do whether they're warlocks or not. Warlocks show a greater need which makes sense with how they, uh, operate," she said when a woman walked past us trying to console her toddler.

"That's what I've been told. Thanks." The vice was back around my chest. Jean-Marc was a good kid and loving, unlike his father. He didn't deserve to have this additional burden on him while trying to go to college.

"You know, you can use a Lodestone and fill it with power. That way, the mage would have a source on him at all times. He wouldn't need to drain it unless there aren't any ley lines near. One wouldn't be necessary in a place like Camden. That's one of the reasons the Pleiades settled here hundreds of years ago."

If I could get a Lodestone, I wouldn't have to worry constantly about Jean-Marc going to the Piney Wood Park to recharge. "Where can I get a Lodestone? And what were the other reasons she came here? It seems like a remote section to settle in and not easily accessible by very many witches."

Tarja drilled into my head that I needed to be open to helping all over the Eastern half of the country because that was my territory.

Clio stepped around her cart and got closer when a family exited the store and started heading our way. "The Witch Trials made her flee Salem. Anyway, I'd bet Hattie had a Lodestone in her supplies. If not, visit The Last Spell and see Clara."

"I know, Clara. Thank you for sharing that information with me. I still have a lot to learn. It was nice to see you," I said, moving toward the store.

"I never stop learning, so don't feel bad. Take care." Clio's shoes clicked as she resumed her race. The woman was intense, that was for sure.

Focused and ready, I pulled out the list my mother made me. I tried to get her to text it to me, but she was old school and wrote everything down. I started in the produce aisle and went right for the russets.

I was used to buying five or six, so the ten-pound bag my mom told me to get astounded me. I hadn't paid any attention to how much food was cooked each day. When I thought about it, I realized it had to be a lot, and my mom had taken over the grocery shopping to give Layla more time to help me.

There were six adults plus Tarja and Mythia. Sometimes seven if Aidoneus was there for dinner. Now we had a ghoul that ate her weight in meat each day. I had no idea what to do with her, so it seemed she'd be with us for a while. There was no way I could send her away when she had nowhere to go.

Veggies checked off the list, I hit the meat section next. I was tempted to ask the butcher if he had a side of beef but bit my tongue. He'd laugh and think it a joke when I was serious.

I snagged three of the biggest packages of baby back ribs I could, then searched for the stew meat. I tossed in five roasts, several pork tenderloins, and twenty pounds of other meat.

Next on the list was beef broth, onion powder, bay leaves, Worchester sauce, and french bread. I was reaching for the bottle of sauce when a red flash caught my attention. My magic hummed in the background at all times now. Experience had turned me into a trigger-happy maniac who was just given a new gun to play with. By the grace of newfound luck, I held my witch fire in check.

It wasn't easy with my twitchy nerves. A woman about my mother's age put cans of some vegetables in her cart halfway down the aisle, but there was nothing else. The magical world was turning me into a loon.

I snagged the bottle and continued to the next aisle for the broth. When I left the house to go on this seemingly mundane mission, I was stoked and ready for something ordinary. Nothing happened at the grocery store. Right? Wrong.

When I turned down the next funnel of fun, my eyes skipped over the cookies I planned on adding to my cart and landed on the tiny creature that looked like it came out of a cheesy horror movie.

A tiny demon jumped from foot to foot with a smile on

its red face. I blinked and rubbed my eyes. That couldn't be right. There couldn't be a bright crimson demon with a long tail and tiny horns bouncing around like a toddler hopped up on lollipops and soda.

The thing blew a raspberry, spit flying off the black tongue before it turned and darted away. Meat forgotten, the hold on my magic vanished in an instant. Energy crackled between my fingers like lightning bugs dancing along my skin.

I'd have marveled if I wasn't too busy chasing the damn thing through the store. I made it to the end of the aisle to see it toss a bottle of wine. I didn't bother seeing where it landed and followed it into the back of the store. Thankfully, there were no mundies watching me. I had to believe that they couldn't see the imp, either. There would be screaming and running if they did.

I cursed at the funhouse of food products laid out before us. The demon was five feet away, staring at the shelves lined up like soldiers awaiting their next order. The expression on his face was one of awe and anticipation.

"*Prohibere.*" The spell left my lips right as the little demon jumped to the top of the shelves. There wasn't enough bleach in the world to cleanse my eyes when his twig waved at me as he soared through the air then slapped his berries when he landed. The thing could pass for a third leg.

Ugh. It was no wonder my spell fizzled. No way to concentrate. His spit hit me this time when he stuck his tongue out and blew it at me. I rolled my eyes and started into the maze. The soldiers soared over fifteen feet into the air with their burdens and made it difficult to see the little red bastard.

Thankfully, he was louder than a herd of elephants charging through a forest, and I was able to make my way through the obstacles to the back loading dock. Large steel doors blocked the way, forcing him to dash through the single metal door for employee use.

Without losing momentum, I was through the door and throwing my hand up to block the bright sun from blinding me. The rash move cost me, and the tiny demon caught me off guard and knocked me off the platform and to the ground six feet below.

The breath whooshed out of me, and my back protested wildly. That was going to hurt later. The demon landed on me and jumped from foot to foot, laughing before blowing another raspberry.

His spit burned my eyes, making my vision blurry. His weight disappeared, and I found myself skidding along the ground as a foot kicked my side. I curled into a ball and cried out when something cracked inside my chest.

Now I was practically blind and unable to breathe. "*Protego.*" I tried to picture the bubble of protection surrounding me as I rolled to my hands and knees. A foot connected with my chest again.

Expecting the attack, I had tensed, and my hands were already in motion. I grabbed hold of something far slimmer than I expected. The smell hit me then, too. It could have been the back alley, but I doubted that was the only urine source or rotten food.

The body landed on me, making pain bloom in my torso. Stars winked in my blurry eyes. God, that hurt. I needed to strike out and hurt this guy. I brought my knee up and tried to grab for his face.

My hand slid over a jagged horn before I pressed some-thing squishy. Going for broke, I shoved my thumb in and slammed my knee home. My knee bounced off something solid, but the creature roared above me.

My vision started to clear, and I saw a shooting star coming for me. My arms lifted on instinct and were crushed against my upper chest. The star-struck home and sliced through my chest.

Pain exploded in my chest, and I blinked at the grey-skinned demon that had one eye missing. I couldn't take a full breath as something wet trickled down my side. I was bleeding. So much for my shield.

I tried to calm my mind enough to cast a spell when I heard shouting. The demon took off like it had been shot out of a cannon. My head was fuzzy, and I couldn't manage to enchant myself.

I had no doubt he would be back to finish me off. I gasped, blackness crowding in around the edges when I tried to sit up. Suddenly, a middle-aged man with a receding hair-line and slight paunch jutting over his belt hovered over me with a cell phone to his ear.

"It's okay. I'm getting help. You're going to be fine." The worry on the guy's face matched the frantic way his free hand waved over my body.

My eyes slipped closed. I hated to break it to the guy, but I wasn't going to be alright. I was losing blood, and I was positive that whatever had hit me came close to my aorta. It hadn't cut it, or I would already be dead, but my situation was far from okay.

My head lolled to the side, and I saw a woman with long, black hair and piercing grey eyes standing next to a dark van. The dark aura surrounding her was matched by the hatred in her eyes. My body shuddered as evil energy surged into me. My magic shoved it out the second I felt something sting the flesh close to my heart.

It was eerily similar to Myrna's magic. This woman was a Tainted witch and casting spells. I tried to open my mouth and tell the guy to get out of there, but nothing came out. The darkness spread, and my eyes slipped closed. I heard the guy's frantic voice and sirens before everything went blank.

* * *

I GASPED THEN GROANED when awareness came to. The surface beneath me was soft, which meant I wasn't on the ground behind the store anymore. I cracked an eye open, afraid I was going to be looking into those angry grey eyes.

The bright fluorescent overhead lights were a particularly brutal form of torture I knew all too well. My heart paused before it battered my rib cage then settled in a regular rhythm. This was my world. I knew hospitals.

"Phoebe! You're awake." My mom's anxious voice made me turn my head.

Nana was sitting in a chair behind her while Stella and Aidoneus hovered like sentinels in the doorway. My daughter was next to my mom and holding my hand. I squeezed her fingers, and a tear slipped down her cheek. The glass slider was open. I was in an ICU ward. The nurse brushing past my friends didn't come as a surprise.

"Hey," I croaked and lifted a hand to my throat. The pain and swelling were common for what I'd been through after being rescued. I knew what the nurse was about to share with me. I'd been intubated while they operated. "Did it hit my aorta?"

The nurse smiled and shook her head. "I'm Amanda, and I'll be your nurse tonight. Your mom told me you were a charge nurse. Apparently, a good one. No, it missed it, but it hit the celiac artery. Dr. Shaw did a vascular graft repair. The fact that you're already awake is a good sign."

"Did he find a bullet? The attack happened so fast I didn't see what hit me." The last part was for my friends and family. Of which two more played helicopter parent behind Stella and Aidoneus. Tears filled my eyes when I saw Layla and Tsekani.

Jean-Marc arrived with a tray of drinks. "Mom! It's good to see you awake. What did I miss?"

"Nothing, yet," Amanda said. "I was just about to start my exam. There was no bullet. You were stabbed, not shot." Hmmm. I thought I saw something silver, but who the heck knows. It was chaotic, and I was being attacked. "You have a median sternotomy incision with wire closures. You know the drill, I'm sure. For those of you without a nursing degree, we need to watch for infection around the stitches. Your vitals look good. How is your pain level?"

Amanda crossed to my other side and lifted one side of the dressing without exposing my chest to the rest of the room. She gently replaced the taped side on my skin.

"Pain's not too bad yet. I could use some ice chips for my throat, though."

Jean-Marc put the paper cups on the rolling table. "I'll grab some for you."

"Your incision looks great so far. There's some redness and swelling, which is to be expected. Your vitals are better than we anticipated, given the injury. Press this button if you need anything. And, I'm sure you know how to use this plunger if your pain gets worse."

I nodded my head. "I do, thank you." Amanda was gone with a promise to be back.

"What happened?" Nana demanded when we were alone again.

Jean-Marc returned with a cup of ice that Aidoneus took from him. It was unnerving to have the son of Hades standing on one side of a hospital bed right after I had my chest cracked open and repaired.

"I saw a small red demon in Hannaford while I was shopping. I couldn't allow it to harm anyone in the store, so I chased it to the back of the store, where I walked right into a trap and was attacked. There was a witch there with black hair and grey eyes. I was incapacitated before I could do anything."

Aidoneus gave me a scoop of ice. "Did the creature have a tail and act almost childish?"

"Yeah," I said around a mouth of melting ice. The cool liquid soothed my irritated esophagus. "It blew raspberries and jumped around the storeroom like a monkey."

Aidoneus's brow furrowed. "It was an imp."

Phoebe! My battered heart jumped in my chest when her voice entered my mind. *"Don't ever chase demons when you're alone again. You should have known it was a trap. I can't lose you. I just started liking you."*

"I'm sorry, Tarja. I didn't think about the possibility of it being a trap. The demon seemed more like a nuisance than a threat, so I followed him. I won't do that again."

Aidoneus brushed the hair off my forehead. "Imps are trouble makers. They prefer to go in, wreak havoc and get out, leaving you to clean up the mess. When tasked, they will attack, so don't assume they won't ever hurt you."

An elephant was sitting on a Medieval spiked ball mace on my chest. Holy crap, balls, I should have been nicer to my patients because this was freaking brutal. "Trust me, I will call you next time."

My mom leaned over and kissed my forehead. "You need to be careful, sweetheart. I made you from scratch and put a lot of blood, sweat, and tears into you."

Jean-Marc sat at the foot of the bed and rubbed one of my calves. "Yeah, mom. That scared the crap out of us."

"It scared us all. Clio is on her way to give you a healing session. I want you in better condition before you go to sleep."

I did, as well. I didn't like thinking my celiac artery had to be patched. That was a severe injury. "It might be difficult to explain to the doctors why I recover so quickly."

Aidoneus frowned. "I don't give a crap what any doctor

says or asks. I will erase their memories if I have to. I am with Tarja on this. I want you healed."

I liked hearing how much he cared, a bit too much. My eyes got heavy, and my mind fuzzy. Morphine was a wonderful thing. The pain of talking weighed on me. I closed my eyes and heard my family discuss ways to locate the witch I'd seen and drifted off with Tarja purring in the back of my mind. I'd survived the worst attack yet and was determined not to let this scare me away from taking action. I was the Pleiades witch of the Eastern United States and becoming a damn good detective.

CHAPTER 9

a noise jolted me awake, and I cried out when my body went to jack-knife into a sitting position. My skull slammed back on the paper-thin cotton, trying its hardest to pass for a pillow. I laid stock still, catching my breath and waiting to see if the worst of the pain would pass or if I'd need some more morphine.

In the six, or so hours that had passed since I'd woken up from surgery, I had used it twice. I preferred not to use it at all. The regular doses made everything look shiny and bright. I didn't need the world to turn into a rainy day in Seattle. The way things had gone over the past few days, I needed to be as clear-headed as possible.

The ache in my chest had a piercing heartbeat all its own. Clio was beside herself, knowing I was attacked shortly after she'd seen me earlier at the store. The nurses were shocked by how good my incision looked. I told Clio to heal the internal wounds as much as possible, focusing on the patched artery.

It was clear within seconds the injury was beyond what Clio could manage, but she assured me the patch was fully healed. The cuts and sutures were another thing altogether. She'd managed to knit the edges of the internal tissues and not much more. It was enough. It made me feel better knowing I wasn't in danger of blowing a patch.

A scratching noise made my exhausted heart jump into high gear as if the green flag had just been lowered and it was determined to win the hundred-meter-sprint regardless of recent surgery.

Without moving my chest too much, I scanned the room. In the corner of the ceiling, close to the closed bathroom door, there was an imp, as Aidoneus called them. The creature's claws were embedded into the plaster as it hung upside down.

Seeing I was awake, it launched itself at me. I was a sitting duck. Refusing to be caught off-guard, I cast a full-body condom, making it an impenetrable shield that surrounded me. "*Clipeum.*"

The tiny demon bounced off the shield and shrieked as it launched through the air. The creek of the bathroom door was an ominous bell tolling the end of my rest. Curse words flew around my grey matter like angry bees protecting their hive. It took all of my energy to sit up and swing my feet off the bed.

The imp that prowled from the bathroom had intact horns with sharp tips that could probably cut through stone. Once my head stopped spinning, I lowered myself until my feet landed on the cold floor. Good thing I wasn't trying to be sneaky. The plastic mattress crinkled and made more noise than riders on a roller coaster. The temperature drop jolted me and erased some of the sedative effects of the pain killers.

I heard movement behind me but couldn't swivel fast enough to keep the first imp from landing on my shoulders. Claws raked over the back of my neck, telling me my shield slipped. I reinforced the Teflon coating me, and the imp scrambled to maintain his hold.

With one hand on the bed, I shook my shoulders. In my head, I imagined myself flinging the tiny demon across the room, so he collided with his compatriot. In reality, it seemed like I had a seizure and didn't so much as a jostle the imp clinging to my back.

The imp in the bathroom blew a raspberry and charged right at me. "What do you want? Aidoneus is going to kill you both when he gets a hold of you."

Apparently, I needed to up my game. They laughed, not frightened of my threat in the least. My foot sailed through the air on instinct and connected with the imp's chest. In Wily Coyote fashion, he twisted and turned as he soared then went splat. An outline of his body marred the white wall with a smear of black blood where the head was.

I was learning to defend myself and use my magic bit by bit, and it was paying off. My body knew what to do, even when my sluggish mind refused to catch up. I needed to contain these assholes and call Aidoneus.

Reaching over my shoulder, I grabbed hold of a long skinny appendage. I laughed as I considered what it could be but didn't let the possibilities stop me from yanking it off me. The imp broke free of my shield with a sucking sound, and I held it out in front of me by the tail.

Grabbing the hospital phone attached to my bed, I dialed a nine then input Aidoneus's number. I should have asked for my cell phone. I shook the demon, making it let out an eep sound.

The phone vanished from my ear, and the second imp tried to claw my arm. Plastic hit the floor, and I wiggled my arm back and forth rapidly to dislodge the class five clinger.

"Hello. Phoebe, is that you?" Hearing his deep voice soothed the panic rising along with my blood pressure.

"Aidon. Imps in. My room." The sentence was disjointed as I gasped more than spoke it. Aidon replied, but it was lost to the sudden ringing in my ears.

My head was so full of cotton it made a better pillow than the one on the plastic bed. I tried to pay attention and figure out how the heck they'd gotten into my room. Of course, those buggers were wily and could go anywhere unseen by mundies. Trying to figure it out at the moment was a waste of energy.

My shield slipped, and claws dug into my arm. I reacted before the second sharp nail cut through my skin. I watched the blood well for a second before I tossed the imp with sharp horns. It was like throwing darts, and he ended up stuck in the drywall.

The reach around for the other one was a lesson in pain, but I persisted and sent him in the direction of his friend. The second imp landed on the back of the first then slid down. It grabbed hold of the tail and hung there like a demonic chandelier earring.

"*Sileo.*" I cast a be still spell but wasn't sure it would actually work. My head was going to explode any second, and the elephant on my chest was trying to lose weight by doing calisthenics on my newly sutured sternum.

There was a garbled sound before the tiny demons puffed up like a hot Cheeto, then exploded like a firework on the fourth of July. Red sprayed around the room, followed by bits of flesh. I gagged and bent over to throw up when a piece of demon landed in my open mouth.

The door opened, and I turned my head to see Aidoneus enter the room with wide eyes. "What the hell happened? Are you alright?" I wiped the vomit off my mouth with the back of my hand and stood up straight.

He crossed to me and scooped me into his arms without concern for the mess covering me. "I tried to make the imps stop moving and clawing me. Instead, they exploded. My head and chest are killing me, so my magic is wonky." I grabbed the pole with my IV bags when he started walking to the bathroom.

Aidon set me down next to the toilet with a smile on his face. "I shouldn't have doubted you could handle them. Although, this isn't what I expected to encounter when I raced over here. You get in the shower while I get the nurses and orderlies to clean the mess."

"I hope you can erase this bloody mess from their minds. This will freak the mundies the hell out." I would have quit if I walked in a room looking like this.

Aidoneus nodded with a smile. "I'm not all-powerful, but I can handle that."

Relief flooded me. "Thank you. Oh, and on second thought, have them call the building maintenance. They will need a ladder to reach the ceiling. Then come back. I'm not very steady on my feet." Butterflies tried to take flight, but they'd been drugged along with me and barely managed to hop.

Aidoneus cupped my cheek and pressed a kiss to my forehead before leaving the restroom and closing the door. I twisted the faucet to hot then unsnapped the gown at the shoulders. I had to take a break before undoing the back ties. The injuries and healing process had zapped me of all my strength.

Stepping under the hot spray, I sighed and dropped my head back to get my hair wet. I should have capped off my IV, but I didn't have the saline. The Tegaderm covered the insertion site. Typically, we add more to ensure it didn't get wet. The chance of infection increases significantly if it does. There was no way I was leaving demon blood on me. I cast a shield spell around the IV and scrubbed my body clean.

* * *

AIDONEUS HELD the door to his house open with a shy smile. It had been five days since I was attacked. Jean-Marc had returned to college, taking a Lodestone with him. I'd been out of the hospital for a day when Aidoneus came by and asked me to come for dinner.

Nana and my teenaged daughter teased me endlessly when I'd agreed. I almost said no. I needed the rest to continue healing. My desire to find that one great love in my life is what made me go. At that point, I didn't know if it was Aidoneus or not, but I wanted to find out.

That man made me feel things I never had before. When I met Miles, I was a giddy freshman in college. I was attracted to him and found a common interest in the medical field. Still, I never got breathless, nor did my stomach do summer-saults while my heart beat against my chest wall.

I whistled as we walked inside. Being the son of Hades had its perks. That was the only reason he could buy the house to the left of mine, close, and move in all within a few days.

"How did you manage all this? I've been in Hattie's house for six months, and I still have my clothes in boxes in the closet."

Aidoneus chuckled and nudged me forward with his hand at the small of my back. "It pays to have money. I paid for people to pack up the former residents and put their stuff in storage while they figured out their next move. Another group of movers was unloading the moving van full of my furniture an hour after closing."

The entryway was open to a formal living room on the left and looked like a music room on the right. The floors were dark wood, and the walls were shades of grey. I was surprised to see antique furniture in the formal areas. I expected black leather for some reason.

I sucked in a breath at the romantic scene he set up in his living room. The soft brown couches were pushed against the walls and a large mattress covered in a dark teal comforter and dozens of pillows. The other furniture off to the sides was as informal and comfy as the couch.

Candles and a roaring fire illuminated the low coffee table full of fruit, cheeses, meats, and crackers. He gestured for me to sit in the middle of the bed. It felt decadent and naughty to lounge on a plush mattress on the floor.

"Because you are still healing, I figured this would be the most comfortable for you."

I lifted one eyebrow as I slipped off my shoes then climbed into the middle of the mattress. It was the size of Texas and softer than a cloud. "Uh-huh. The fact that it's the perfect place to get me into your bed had nothing to do with it?"

Aidoneus shrugged his shoulders with a wicked smile. "I won't apologize for wanting you. You're a beautiful woman. But I will never pressure you into anything you aren't ready for. It will be your decision when we finally make love."

I leaned over and reached for the kiwi. Aidoneus grabbed two platters, one of which held the fruit and placed it in front of me. His heady masculine scent teased my nose and made me want to move closer and inhale.

He kicked off his shoes and joined me on the bed. It wouldn't take long for me to tear off my clothes and beg him to take me. As a distraction, I popped a cube of fruit into my mouth and laid against the pillows. There were so many that it was like sitting up in a fluffy chair. It was so comfortable I could melt into the cushions.

"You're awfully confident we will end up in bed together."

Aidoneus held up a piece of watermelon. I opened my

mouth and bite off part of the crisp fruit. "I hate to point out the obvious, but we already are."

I choked as I chewed and nearly inhaled the sweet flesh rather than swallowing it. "You have a point. I haven't done this with anyone since marrying my ex-husband over twenty years ago, so you'll have to be patient with me."

Aidoneus leaned over me and caged me with his body. "It's been longer than that for me. I worried this was too much and not enough at the same time."

There was no way I heard him right. "What do you mean it's been longer?" Why was I smiling like a loon in reaction to that?

The answer hit me like a lightning strike. He's older than dirt, literally. I assumed he'd slept with more women than were alive on the planet, so it was a relief I wasn't going to be following in the heels of a supermodel or something.

Aidoneus pressed a kiss to the corner of my mouth. "I mean, I haven't been with a woman for almost a century. Watching my uncles have affairs and ruin lives with their dalliances made me hesitate to engage in any of my own, even though I wasn't married. I've always believed I'd find someone that made my blood sing and owned my every desire."

He had my body heating and my arousal building. I was panting like a french bulldog in hundred-degree tempera-tures. "That's funny. I was just thinking the same thing."

His lips were distracting as he kissed a path down the side of my neck. I tilted my head, giving him more access. I put my hands over his when he went for the buttons on my top. The wire sutures came out this morning, and I was extremely self-conscious of that fact. I had more lumps on my body than the Rocky Mountains and stretch marks bigger than Interstate 10. Still, I was most nervous about him seeing the sternotomy scar.

Okay, so it wasn't the scar itself. My scars were badges of honor. They told my story better than a Pulitzer Prize-winning author could. It was about my boobs. When they cracked my chest open, it caused the girls to droop even more. Besides that, no one had seen me naked aside from Miles for the last two decades.

I wanted to be as confident with him seeing me as I was with facing demons and casting spells. Unfortunately, I was shaking and sweating while keeping my gaze focused on the big picture window and stormy seas outside.

Aidon lifted his head and sat back on his heels. He tugged his sweater over his head and tossed it aside. His pecs flexed as he moved. His skin was dark copper, and his musculature perfect. The scars marring his chest and arms surprised me. I didn't think a god would scar.

My hand lifted and traced over a large gash right over where his heart pounded as fast as mine. I smiled, knowing he was as nervous as I was and it eased my nerves. "I'm perfectly imperfect. I've got scars and at least fifteen or twenty extra pounds. I don't want to have sex with you tonight, but an orgasm or ten wouldn't be unwelcome."

He threw his head back and laughed. The humor and desire in his eyes when he focused on me emboldened me. I tugged the shirt over my head, getting stuck halfway. He helped and tossed it aside while his eyes remained glued to my chest.

He leaned down and kissed a path down my scar. He reached behind me and unbuttoned my bra but didn't remove it. Instead, his mouth kept moving over my flesh, licking and teasing me into a frenzy.

The pain was practically gone. I'd get twinges every once in a while. What really lingered was the fatigue. I was still so damn exhausted. At that moment, I felt nothing but pleasure and mounting desire.

My back arched, and I tugged one bra strap off then the other. Aidoneus stopped and looked at me so long I started to squirm. Before I managed to get away, he had my yoga pants off and on the floor, along with my underwear.

My face flushed as he looked me over. I'd been self-conscious ever since I had my kids. And I was with him, until his sapphire lifted to mine. He saw me and wanted me anyway. There was no hint he didn't like my love handles or the scars my kids left on my stomach.

"I want to see you, now."

He moved so fast I couldn't follow the movement. His jeans were off, and he knelt naked in front of me. I got a second before he pressed his body to mine and started kissing me in earnest.

His erection slid through my arousal and almost had me climaxing right then. Rational thought fled to be replaced by sensual need. My hips thrust up and rubbed my core against his shaft.

He was moving with me. His mouth lowered to my breasts, and he sucked on one of my nipples. No one had ever made my body fly to the edge so fast. Or been so gentle with me. Every move he made was designed to give me pleasure while making sure not to open my chest.

I cried out his name within seconds and wasn't surprised when he followed a second later. I collapsed against the pillow smiling up at him. He cupped my cheek and pressed a gentle kiss to my lips. "I'm going to devour you now that the edge has been taken off."

I trusted this man to treat me with care and not hurt me. It was more than I'd ever hoped to have again, and I was going to enjoy myself. "Who said the urgency was gone?"

I laughed when he growled and claimed my mouth in a passionate kiss. Looked like I wasn't going to be getting any sleep tonight.

CHAPTER 10

"*T*his feels like an extension of Nimaha," Layla observed as we walked to Aidoneus's land and the site where we were going to open the Hellmouth.

Adrenaline fueled my steps. I was anxious to get this process done. With the way demons had been popping up all over the place, it was time to do more to control their presence. Thankfully, Aidoneus had convinced Thnos and my best friend Fiona in Cottlehill Wilds to open a Hellmouth there, as well. Unfortunately, the other Pleiades were still on the fence about their areas.

Demonic activity in Luciana Umbra's territory was only now seeing an uptick. Where she was in Italy, it was far enough away from England and Fiona that she was shielded from the worst of it and was content to watch what happened with me first. However, she seemed open to discussing more about Stuleros and having her familiar, Zephyrus meet up with Tarja.

None of the other Pleiades had yet responded. Tarja suggested we open the Hellmouth without waiting because I'd been attacked countless times and nearly died. My stomach did flips as we got closer to the designated area. I hadn't seen Aidoneus since our night together. After giving me more orgasms than I could count, he'd spent the next three days in the Underworld preparing for the ritual.

Refocusing on the conversation, I flared my magical senses to see what Layla was talking about. "Is that because I cast protection spells over the property? I did it like I did with Hattie's land."

"It's your land now. You must fully claim it."

I looked down at my familiar as she walked next to me. "I have fully claimed it, Tarja."

One of her eyes focused on me with an intensity that made me jumpy. *"You still see it as Hattie's. The house, too. The magic senses that, which is part of the reason you struggle for control."*

I flushed and focused on the path in front of me as I thought about her comment. I had a difficult time thinking of it as mine. It was Hattie's, and it felt wrong for me to claim it when I owed her so much for giving it to me.

Denial choked me, making my heart race for a reason other than sexy thoughts about Aidon. "I see your point. The magic is mine. As is Nimaha and the inhabitants that live on my property. I will always honor Hattie and am grateful to her, but it's mine now, and I need to make it mine."

Energy made the wind bluster around us, sending my hair flying in every direction. The air smelled of jasmine and vanilla. Energy poured through me and flared out from there. I felt it tickle the leaves in the trees and spread throughout my property. Pixies flitted around their mound. Shifters burrowed into their dens, sat up, and took notice.

I'd felt the connection from the moment I cast the protections months ago. This only solidified it. I hadn't realized there'd been an edge to the bond lately. Now that I was paying attention, I felt how it had scratched at the back of my mind until it was gone.

It had been waiting for me to fully claim it in my heart and make it mine, rather than carrying it for Hattie. It was funny how I never considered that I had been carrying this burden for her and been trying to live up to her image. I still wanted to make her proud, but this was all about me and my magic now.

This power was nothing like it had been when Hattie possessed it. It changed the second she gave it to me like it should. I just needed to realize that and accept it.

"Now, you're ready to open the Hellmouth. You have the full power of the land behind you."

I couldn't believe I hadn't had access to all of the power before now. Anger and frustration bubbled beneath the surface. "Why didn't you mention anything before? I would have done something sooner."

"You wouldn't have seen what I was talking about before now. You believed you'd claimed us fully. I'm connected to you. I know you've seen me as Hattie's familiar and a gift she gave you. Both are true, but it kept you from owning me in the real sense. Now, I'm yours because you realized the truth and took what belongs to you rather than continuing to see it as Hattie's. Now we might actually be able to deal with the spirits haunting Stuleros."

"You're right, and I had no idea the subtle difference existed, let alone that it was causing problems."

My sixteen-year-old daughter gasped and clasped her chest. "We need to write this down. She admitted she was wrong." Layla laughed but kept her mouth shut.

I rolled my eyes at her drama. "I never said I was wrong, just that Tarja was right. Anyway, do you know what I should expect with this Hellmouth process?"

"No idea. This is beyond my wheelhouse."

"But not beyond mine," Aidoneus said as we reached the

94

patch of land nestled in the trees that he'd picked out for the Hellmouth. It was surrounded by evergreens, and the ground was covered in ivy and various other lush plant life. "Together, we will cast a net that will sit between the realms. I need to summon a higher demon to open the veil. When I do that, I need you to cast a doorway tied to the net."

He'd gone over it with me, and now that it was here, I wanted to throw up. I wasn't sure I could handle this process. He had the hard part controlling then sacrificing the higher demon he called through while I only had to cast the doorway. Nothing in my life had been simple or easy. The thought of this going wrong when it involved a higher demon was terrifying.

Layla clapped my back, dragging me out of the spiral. "You've got this, Pheebs."

"She's right, mom. Don't be afraid." Nina hugged me, grounding me in my magic and family.

The hum of an engine announced the arrival of my mom and Nana. Tsekani had driven them on the ATV because the trek would have been too much for Nana. I wanted her to stay safe at home, but she refused to miss it. I'd agreed because I needed their support.

Nana stopped short and started moving back to the ATV before she paused. "What the hell? Why can't I approach?"

"It's safest between the trees. The demon won't be able to reach you there." When Aidoneus said that, I poked at the area and felt the hum of magic. There was a darker edge to it that was harsh and biting. Power, my senses screamed at me, urging me to run for the hills. Sheer force of will kept me in the middle of the small clearing. Everyone else, including my familiar, stood outside the circle.

"What spell is around this area?" I couldn't pick out the nuances. I wasn't that advanced yet.

Aidoneus shrugged. "I spent the day laying the blood

runes for containment and aversion. We don't need more than fifteen feet, so I used the natural border of the trees." If he wasn't a god, the use of Blood magic would have Tainted him. Without them, a mortal could stumble upon the Hell-mouth and open it without knowing what they were doing.

I joined Aidon in the center of the clearing and extended my hands. One of his eyebrows quirked, but he took them in his. "This isn't part of the ritual."

I shrugged my shoulders. "I don't care. I am making our bond part of the process. Touching you connects me to your magic, so I can tie my spell to what you are doing without much effort."

The corner of his mouth twitched as he inclined his head. "Let's begin."

I nodded and closed my eyes. It was easier to shut out my surroundings. I focused on what we'd talked about. When we settled on the approach, I'd researched strong metals and decided on using osmium in my thoughts. I wanted it to be impenetrable.

Keeping the osmium screen in mind, I wrapped it around the world. I wanted the net to stand between the Under-world and Earth. Energy tingled where my flesh connected with Aidoneus. "*Laqueum*," I said at the same time Aidoneus chanted in a language I didn't recognize.

Magic burst from the two of us like an atom bomb deto-nating. If Aidoneus hadn't held my hands, I'd have been blown into one of the trees. For a second, while the energy seeped out of us and spread to encompass the land, I was able to sense Aidoneus's awe at doing magic with me.

The deep connection cut off just as I picked up his desire. Good thing, or I wouldn't have been able to continue with the process. I sucked in a breath, and my stomach grumbled when I smelled black licorice.

It reminded me of one of my favorite candies and Vietnamese food since they used anise in many of their dishes. A mixture of herbs replaced that scent, making me think of pasta sauce.

Light flashed behind my closed lids, making me crack them open. White, blue, green, red, and orange lights filled the clearing. It colored my family sitting with wide eyes outside the circle.

Aidoneus let go of my hands and cut his palms with a claw that extended from his pointer finger. I'd never seen him in his godly form, but that made me wonder if he was demonic in appearance.

He dripped the blood in a design on the ground. Something possessed me to grab his hand and slice through my palm. He gasped and stared at me for several seconds while I dripped my blood on the top of his.

"What the hell are you doing. No! You're going to Turn." I blocked Tarja's voice from my mind. I wasn't going to Turn. Aidoneus's magic protected me, and this was the way I would successfully open the doorway.

I wasn't sure where that knowledge was coming from, but my gut was far louder since my earlier claim. Aidoneus blinked and persisted. We continued the spell, with my hand moving with his. It almost felt like he was stroking my skin.

I shuddered and reveled in the bond with him. I felt the second the magic reached its apex. I imagined a circle of darkness with a massive silver lid covering it. Aidoneus held his arms out to his sides and chanted in the same language.

A dark circle started forming in the middle of the clearing and made us take several steps back as it grew in size. When lightning crackled in the middle of the abyss, I saw countless hands ending in claws reaching for freedom. Some had red skin, some had grey, and others had green flesh with sores.

The worst part of that moment was the stench. Brimstone came to mind, but rotten eggs was a more apt description. It reminded me of when my kids had gotten some flavored jelly beans and made me eat a rotten egg one. I'd thrown up for hours after.

Bile pummeled the back of my throat, and I swallowed hard, trying to force it into submission. I was saved from focusing on the battle when I saw it was my turn. A massive beast with greenish-grey skin emerged above the rest of the demons.

In my mind, the osmium net connected to a doorway. "*Ostium*," I chanted when his chest was above the opening.

The light was so bright I had to turn away and cover my eyes. When I turned back several seconds later, there were still demons clawing their way out. A ten-foot-tall monster with a misshapen head and sharp teeth was snarling at Aidoneus.

The smell threatened to undo me. Good thing I was so focused on the lights fluttering through the clearing and the magic flowing from Aidoneus. The demon was much taller as he towered over the son of Hades. One word from Aidon, and the creature was on his knees, the color draining from his distorted face.

In a move so fast that I almost missed it, Aidoneus called a sword and slashed through the demon's neck. Its shocked expression lasted for a second before the head toppled to the side. Blood spurted from the stump then the body landed with a thud.

The plants withered where the blood spread. I quickly cast a spell to keep the damage to a confined radius. "*Circulus autem containment.*" The liquid hit a barrier but didn't go further.

I stumbled as the energy drained from me. I landed on a knee and dug my fingers into the ground, feeling for the net and the doorway. The power sang to me immediately.

Aidoneus listed to one side before he carved a rune on the demon's body and said another chant.

A column of black lightning shot into the sky. I prayed mundies couldn't see that, or we would have visitors soon. It vanished a few seconds later and the area hummed with power that told me we'd done it.

"It worked," I observed.

He bent over and braced his hands on his knees. "It did. The Hellmouth is in place."

"*Don't ever do that again, Phoebe.*" I'd never heard so much anger from my familiar.

I turned to Tarja as I climbed to my feet. "I will do what it takes to protect my land and my family. You need to have faith in me. I was following my gut. The spell wouldn't have worked if I wasn't tied to the initial phase. I was never in danger when I used the Blood magic because I tied into Aidon's god powers."

"I told you she knew what she was doing," Nana chided my familiar.

I smiled, standing taller with Nana's belief in me. "Look, Tarja. I get your concern but know I would never do anything that would cause me to become Tainted. But I will not ask you for permission before casting spells."

"*I appreciate knowing you weren't giving into temptation. It took me by surprise, but you guys managed to create the doorway. I can feel it from here. At least now we should have a reprieve from demonic activity.*"

Aidoneus shook his head from side to side. "You are saved from new demons crossing through anywhere in Phoebe's area. The net spans the realm, but there are weak spots where the other Pleiades haven't opened a Hellmouth."

I shrugged my shoulders. "It's harder for them. It makes it all but impossible to summon a higher demon. And witches will need more power to call forth lower-level demons. That's progress. We should go get a drink to celebrate."

My body ached, and exhaustion rode me hard, but this momentous event deserved proper recognition.

"Let's go to my house. I can't leave my property until I locate proper seals, or a witch can undo our work."

My head snapped around, and my mouth fell open. "What do you mean they can undo it? It's supposed to be protected against such an event."

"It will be once we have the seal in place. That's the reason for needing it. Besides, the magic is still settling in and fusing in place. I wouldn't leave while the spot is vulnerable."

I sighed. "I thought there was time to mark the occasion. I'll get to work."

"Nonsense. There's always time to celebrate. Trust me, child, life is too short to let the little things get to you or let the milestones go by unnoticed. Life is meant to be lived. We all want to toast your accomplishment. Some of us doubted you guys would pull it off," Nana called out from her perch on a chair Tsekani had to have brought for her.

"That was you, mother." My mom shook her head with a frown. "But I agree that a drink and piece of cake is in order."

Aidoneus twined his fingers with mine. The cut on my palm throbbed when his skin brushed against the wound. A zing moved through my blood from the spot. The next thing I knew, I felt his pride in my actions.

A smile spread across my face as we walked toward his house. I was happier than I had ever been. As well as sore and tired. Days like this made me love magic even more. I wasn't just fighting against evil but was taking steps to protect others from harm. Few things made me feel this good.

CHAPTER 11

*J*tripped over a branch as I walked through the forest to my house. A hand wrapped around my bicep, keeping me from face planting on the ground. I turned and smiled at Layla. The wolf shifter had become one of my best friends over the last six months and had my back no matter the situation.

Hence the reason she was trekking through the woods with me while my mom, my daughter, Nana, and Tarja drove back on the ATV with Tsekani. "Thanks. My feet refuse to do what I'm telling them."

Layla snorted. "That's because you're exhausted. We should have taken Aidon's car when he offered."

I shook my head vigorously and instantly regretted it. We'd consumed three bottles of wine between the lot of us, and I was certain I had an entire bottle myself. "I needed the cool air to wake me up. I have work to do."

Between the Hellmouth and the wound still healing on my chest, I was in piss-poor shape. I would probably make a mess of the seal, but I felt pressure to complete it quickly. I had a ghoul in my house that I had to help next.

"You're in no shape to do anything tonight. You need to go home and get some sleep." There were dark circles under Layla's eyes, and her steps were slower than usual. I didn't think it was all because she was trying to match my pace.

"Has Selene kept you up at night?" Layla had taken it on herself to watch the ghoul while I did other work.

"She's chatty as all get out, but she hasn't tried to leave or attack me. I feel sorry for her but want to strangle her at the same time. She doesn't seem to need more than a few hours to rest at night while I need my beauty sleep. Not to mention she has seriously cut into my sex life."

"What? Who are you sleeping with?" Layla hadn't talked about being interested in anyone, so this news was a complete shock to me.

"There isn't one guy in particular. The shifters on the property all service each other. Don't give me that look. Wolves are horny by nature, and few of us want to interact with mundies. It's worse for me right now because I'm nearing a heat cycle, and my need is amped up."

"I had no idea you were such a hussy. You never talk about it."

Layla laughed at me. "As if you have any room to talk. You smelled like sex when you came home from Aidoneus's house the other night. Although, I fully approve. You two have been dancing around each other long enough."

My cheeks heated, and I choked on air for a second. Damn shifter senses. I never considered they could smell what I'd done with Aidon. "We didn't actually have sex."

It was Layla's turn to gape at me. "Wow, you guys created quite the bouquet without consummating the deed. At least you know he's worth a second go. Not many can give a girl multiple orgasms. The ones that can are keepers for sure."

"I'd have to agree with that one. It's a new experience for

me. My ex hadn't given me one for at least a decade. He was a two-pump-chump, as many would say."

I'd let go of my expectations and disappointment. If I hadn't, our marriage would have dissolved much sooner. In hindsight, it had been a mistake to ignore my needs and desires like that. He didn't respect or love me more because of it. Quite the opposite. He saw me as easy to ignore.

"You traded up, that's for sure. I bet he's got some moves. As a god, he must be able to rock your world." Layla's laughter was cut off as her body went sailing through the air.

"What the hell?" I blurted and crouched down to avoid being hit next. My eyes scanned my surroundings. At first, I saw nothing. The feral growl made the hair on my neck stand on end and gave me a direction.

There was a guy, shifter based on how his eyes glowed in the moonlight, hiding between two trees. Blood dripped from his mouth full of sharp teeth. Perhaps it was a vampire.

"What do you want?" I hoped it was easily distracted.

His head never wavered from the direction Layla's body had gone. She was hanging from a broken branch that was poking through her right shoulder. Arms that moonlighted as steel bands wrapped around my torso and pinned my arms to my sides. There was no room to wiggle my way out of the grasp, either.

"I want some of that sweetness I smell." There was no doubt the guy was a shifter. The primal feel of his magic as it brushed against mine told me as much.

Unfortunately, there was an acrid edge to his power that made me recoil. It matched the nauseating smell of garbage that wafted from his body. I wiggled and tried to throw my elbow into his gut but couldn't move.

Within a couple seconds, I had to stop moving. It was adding pressure and lighting my chest on fire. The pressure threatened to turn my heart into a pancake while popping my newly healed incision open.

I lifted my foot and slammed it into the ground with enough force to rattle my teeth. I fought to concentrate on a spell. I wanted him knocked on his ass. Thinking that over and over, I decided to go for it. "*Sternent eum.*"

Some force pulled me to the ground, making me cry out. Crap! I know better than to cast when I'm tired and unable to focus. Based on the pain, I thought my tailbone might have been shattered. That might have slowed him down.

As it was, he stood there for a second wondering where I went before he looked down. Layla saved me from losing a chunk of hair when she cried out. "You'll pay for this asshole."

She pushed against the bark on the tree and fell to the ground with a grunt. The guy raced for her and wrapped a claw-tipped hand around her throat, cutting off her air. And her ability to shift, it seemed. Fur sprouted along Layla's arms, but nothing more happened.

Layal's fingernails shifted, and she raked them across the guy's stomach, leaving four deep furrows. He growled at her, baring his teeth right before he lowered his head and sniffed her neck. "Sweet." I wished the moon wasn't quite so bright. I would have happily missed that sight. My stomach agreed as it churned.

I shuddered as slobber dripped from his sharp canines to her shoulder. She shoved at his chest, pissing him off. She was flying through the air before her shout left her lips. This time she soared right past the tree she'd been impaled on to slam into a boulder the size of Jean-Marc's Hyundai.

The snap that echoed throughout the forest when she impacted made me scramble to her side. I did a combination crab crawl and slither across the forest floor. My tailbone bitched louder than a wailing toddler before making me crumble when I tried to stand up.

A fist connected with my spine, and I flailed on my stomach. I couldn't help but scream. I thought for a split second that he'd snapped my spine because I couldn't feel the pain anymore.

I was relieved when I managed to roll away from him. My foot connected to his furry shin as I moved, and it was his turn to meet the dirt. His snarls were practically all I could hear as I laid there, trying to calm my mind so I could cast a spell.

The feral shifter recovered fast and was getting to his feet. I grabbed his leg and tugged. He fell forward, and I used it to pull myself off the ground. I was glad to note my feet stayed underneath me and the light in the forest was enough for me to see what was going on. This could have been much worse if I couldn't get a good view of what was happening around us.

Layla grunted as she rolled off the rock and hit the ground. I took a step toward her and found an arm winding around my waist. The shifter lifted me off the ground then charged toward Layla.

I beat at his hard muscled leg with my fists, but it did nothing to stop him. Layla yelped when he scooped her up with his other arm. Her legs dangled motionless while she battered her fists into his thighs.

"Are you okay, Layla?"

She shook her head; blood droplets being flung off her scalp in the process. "I think my spine snapped in half. We can't let him take us to his lair. Otherwise, we will never get out of there alive. Ferals are deranged killers."

"That's why he smells so bad." His fur covered arm tightened when I said that. Nothing got through to him, and we were being carried away from my house, which was terrible for us. My head bounced off his thigh and gave me an idea.

I grimaced, then reached over and grabbed his balls and squeezed. I tightened my grip and yanked with all my strength. He yowled and dropped both of us. Thankfully, the landing wasn't as bad this time.

My arms shook as I pushed my torso off the ground. I was about to try and get to my feet when I heard running in the trees surrounding us. Could demons have passed through the portal without Aidon or I knowing?

"Phoebe! Layla!"

"Tsekani!" My heart pounded against my rib cage, jumping like a little kid in an amusement park. Relief was a breath of fresh air, despite the rotting garbage smell emanating from the feral shifter.

"There's a feral here, Tseki," Layla warned through clenched teeth.

"Will shifting heal your spine?" I knew shifting healed many wounds. I just wasn't sure about something so severe.

"No. This one will take time." Layla was pale, and her features were pinched. She was in a lot of pain. I wished I could help her, but I didn't trust my magic to do what I wanted at the moment. I'd had too much wine and was injured and exhausted on top of that.

It was music to my ears a second later when Tsekani screeched as he broke through the trees. He raced to the feral and snatched the shifter by the back of the neck.

"Don't kill him," I shouted. I didn't trust this was an accident. I'd become a target for too many and needed to know if he was sent after me. "I want to ask him some questions."

Tsekani shook his head, his gorgeous features hardening. "That's useless. Ferals are driven by base needs and desires. They're incapable of rational thought, but I'll defer to you,

Pheebs. Brody," Tseki called out, "can you carry Layla back to the house? She's injured her spine."

Brody glowered as he stalked through the shrubs and joined us. I didn't know Tseki's boyfriend very well, but he sure seemed surly. "Can you walk?" The way he snarled at me made me want to shrink away from him.

No way this guy was going to scare me. I glowered right back at him. "As if I'd let you carry me. I'm fine. Be careful with Layla, or you'll have to answer to me. And I guarantee you won't like it."

His eyes widened and flicked to Tsekani, then back to me. I kept my head high as I struggled to get to my feet. My tailbone screamed at me, but I kept it hidden. There was something about not showing a potential enemy weakness, and I didn't trust this guy.

Layla chuckled and broke the tension. "She schooled your grumpy ass, Brody. You need to learn to trust others. Not everyone is like those in your previous pack."

That was interesting. Whatever had happened to this shifter was violent and traumatic. The old me would have felt bad for him and ignored his aggression. Forget that shit. My magical makeover left me with a bad attitude, trust issues, and a healthy glow.

Brody grumbled something in response that I couldn't hear without their superior hearing. Layla's laugh was cut off by a low groan when he scooped her into his arms. "I'll call Clio and have her meet us at the house so she can treat you when we get home." I patted my back pocket for my phone and winced when I felt a crack in the screen. I'd have to get another one. I broke them more often than mechanics had to change tires during the Indy 500.

"There's no need, Pheebs. Layla and I heal faster than other shifters. She'll be walking by the morning," Tsekani explained as he handed me a broken limb to use as a walking stick. This was why I loved him. He silently supported me without giving me grief and was patient with his explanations.

The quiet was tense as we continued walking to my house. It wasn't easy, and I gave up caring about the need to say something. Silence had never been something I tolerated well. It was one reason Miles was always able to throw me off-kilter enough to win our arguments.

This time I couldn't even credit the new me. It was the concentration it required for me to take each step across the uneven landscape. Arrows of fire jabbed my bottom with every step. I practically ran up the steps when we reached the shore, and my yard came into view.

Nina stood in the open back doors. "Get a heating pad ready, Thia. And lay a blanket on the couch, Gammy. Mom and Layla are hurt."

I heard Nana's curse before she shuffled into view behind my daughter. Selene was next to her, biting her thumbnail.

"We ran into a bit of trouble. Do we have a cage in the basement?" I called out as I climbed the stairs leading to my house. Why the hell were there so damn many? I swear there were more now than there had been hours ago when we left.

"We need to build a dungeon below the house with as often as you're running into trouble," Nana replied.

Nina wrapped her arm around me, and I dropped the walking stick on the patio. I swept through the kitchen heading for the living room. No way was I sitting on the hardwood chairs right now.

Brody swept past us and laid Layla on the couch with the fluffy blanket. My mom hovered nearby. "What happened?"

Nina helped me sit in one of the recliners. I jumped out of the seat when I relaxed. "I need a pillow. I think I broke my coccyx."

Nina rushed to the corner where we had a built-in

shelving unit with bins of blankets and pillows on the bottom. She was back with a soft pillow a second later. I sighed as it helped ease the discomfort and pressure on the injury.

"That asshole attacked us," I announced. "Which is why we need a cage."

Tarja jumped on the end table next to me. *"We don't have a cage, but I can put him in a magical coma while you guys heal."*

"That's perfect. I want to know why he attacked us. I don't believe in coincidence anymore."

Tseki nodded his head. "I don't either. It's possible he stumbled onto your land, but it seems awfully convenient. Especially after all you've been through in the past six months."

"I bet it's that Zaleria," Nana announced as she sat in her recliner.

"Chances are you're right, Amelia. She has proven what she is capable of sending other creatures to do her dirty work."

"Maybe she's not as powerful as we think," my mom said as she draped a blanket over Layla's back. "I mean, so far, we haven't seen her do one thing directly to Phoebe."

Mythia fluttered into the room, holding a tray that she set on the coffee table. She handed me three ibuprofen and a glass of ice water. "Have you considered she might not exist? Myrna could have been trying to scare you and get under your skin."

"Thank you for these," I said and popped them in my mouth before taking a drink of water. "It's possible, but my gut tells me she's out there waiting for her chance."

The others started discussing where she could be and what she might do next while Tarja crossed to Tsekani, who was holding the shifter still. She placed her paw on his forehead. The fight left him, and his eyes slipped closed. That was the coolest thing ever. I freaking loved magic.

CHAPTER 12

"What should I expect from this visit?" My gut was full of squirming worms.

I couldn't tell if I wanted to rush home and sit on the toilet until it passed or take an antacid. I was intimately familiar with doubt, trying to get the better of me. Usually, I was able to talk myself through the reasons I was nervous and find evidence to prove why they were nonsense. This time I had no idea what I was about to face, which left me unsettled.

Tsekani glanced around the property. We were in a remote area at the edge of town and parked in front of a massive white house with a wrap-around porch. "Don't stare the alpha down. Make eye contact to acknowledge him, then avert your gaze. You can look back at him, but it will be seen as a challenge if you hold his gaze. We won't be here long enough to worry about the rest."

People prowled out of the surrounding woods, and my heart started hammering in my chest. Tsekani grabbed my arm and dragged me toward the front door, ignoring the growls coming from the darkness surrounding us. With my luck lately, they'd attack us without provocation.

As if this day hadn't been long enough. Why had I decided we needed to deal with the rogue shifter sooner rather than later? I was exhausted. Creating the Hellmouth had taken more out of me than I anticipated.

I felt the physical drain of my energy with every heartbeat. And Layla was still recovering, so Tsekani had to accompany me to the meeting. He was a great friend and asset to our group, but Layla was usually the one to join me on my excursions.

Tsekani lifted his fist and rapped on the door. His knuckles hit the wood surrounding the gorgeous stained-glass window making up the top half of the panel. My heart mimicked the hard tapping. It skipped a beat when a shadow appeared behind the glass.

The door was opened by a stunning woman in her early thirties wearing skin-tight jeans and a t-shirt. Her long blonde hair was pulled into a ponytail. "What can I do for you?" She narrowed serious, brown eyes on us and pursed her lips.

I lifted a hand and let it fall. "I'm Phoebe Duedonne, the new Pleiades, and I'd like to speak to the alpha. We have an issue with a shifter we'd like to discuss."

If my identity or request surprised her, she showed no sign of it. After a silent second, she stepped aside and gestured for us to enter with a flourish of her hand. "He's inside."

Tsekani went in before me, his energy brushing against my shoulder as he passed. I practically stomped on his heels as I followed behind him. There was a wall behind the door, so I was surprised when we turned down a short hall, and the house opened up to an open floor plan.

The energy of those in the room hit me before the sound

and layout registered. At least ten shifters were talking to each other. And, if I had to guess, the entire first floor was one big space. The entrance to the house was a brief affair that served to hide the house from those visiting. There were no walls in the rest of this section.

Stairs leading to a second story were located along the back of the entrance. Along the wall to the right were four couches surrounding a large screen television hanging above a stone fireplace. Then there were three tables with eight chairs surrounding each platform. A kitchen was between the two.

"Alpha," the woman called out. "Phoebe Duedonne and her associate are here to speak with you."

The entire room went silent, and the guy standing at the stove stirring whatever was cooking in the stockpot looked to see us. He had dark brown hair and intense amber eyes. I could see his wolf in his gaze. He turned fully and handed the wooden spoon to a guy next to him. His power surged forward, making Tsekani take a step closer to me.

He was a good-looking man in his late thirties. It wasn't a hardship to avert my gaze and scan the muscular body that moved with grace in our direction. The room remained quiet, waiting to see what we wanted. It was enough to make me twitchy.

"I'm Sullivan, alpha of the Grey Crest pack here in Camden. Let's have a seat." He gestured to one of the tables.

I winced, my hand going to the base of my spine. When the attractive alpha tilted his head and lifted one eyebrow at me in question. "I broke my coccyx when I was attacked by a feral wolf shifter. That's why I'm here. I am hoping you can help me."

He flicked his chin to someone over my shoulder, and the room cleared a second later. Non-verbal communication between shifters was a powerful thing. I'd never seen anyone comply so fast in my life.

"In that case, the sofa will be more comfortable." He guided me in that direction with a hand on my elbow. His smile was one I recognized. It was that of a guy flirting with a woman he thought was pretty. The possibility boosted my self-esteem but didn't perk my interest.

I sat down gingerly while holding my breath. The injury was getting better, but it had only been a couple hours, so it had a long way to go. Tsekani snagged a throw pillow and lifted me, then placed it under me.

"Thanks." Tsekani nodded his head and sat next to me.

The alpha sat on a sofa closest to where we were seated. "What happened? And where?"

Tsekani leaned forward. "A feral wolf attacked Phoebe and one of our associates in the forest near her property. Are any of your shifters missing?"

Sullivan pulled out his phone and typed a text. A responding ding came a second later. "None of my pack members are missing. There isn't another pack within fifty miles of Nimaha, which makes this a concerning development."

"Why? Isn't it possible that they wandered into town?" That seemed plausible to me.

Sullivan shook his head and made a sound of disgust. "And stumbled across you and your friend? That doesn't happen. Rogues steer clear of areas where there's a large pack. I won't tolerate them in my town. The chances of an unattached shifter going mad from moon sickness are far too high."

"What is moon sickness?" If it was what I was thinking, it was most likely what is wrong with the shifter at my house.

"Moon sickness is when shifters go feral. Our primal nature rises to the surface and takes over rational thought.

They are driven by their urges and have no impulse control," the alpha explained.

"I ran across a feral once who was in the process of killing his wife. He was irrational and ranting about needing to teach her a lesson. I found his kids down the road and made sure they got to their aunt," Tsekani said.

Tsekani didn't have to tell me he'd killed the shifter. The thought made me sick. It seemed like a waste of a life. "Isn't there a way to help them?"

Sullivan shook his head from side to side. "If it's early in the moon sickness, an alpha can often pull them back to sanity. If they're too far gone or completely lost to their madness, there's nothing to be done. It sounds like it might be best to put this shifter out of his misery."

I gasped. "How can you say that? There's no way I am going to allow you to kill him until we know more. I came here to ask if you have a cage that can hold him while we try and gather more information."

Sullivan patted my knee, letting his hand linger for longer than necessary, which made me want to squirm in my seat. I didn't, mainly because it would feel like sitting on shards of glass. "You've not been in the magical world long, have you? The story your friend told is one of the nicer ones. I've had to deal with ferals that have massacred small towns. And let's not forget they rape the women while they're at it. I never resort to killing them without first trying to help them. I've saved some, but I cannot allow them to live when so many innocent lives pay the price. It's not worth the risk."

My gut twisted into one giant knot. I swallowed down the bile playing tonsil hockey in the back of my throat. "I was a mundie seven months ago, so yeah. I don't know this world well enough, and I often forget it has nasty consequences. I would love your guidance in dealing with this situation."

"Not many in your position of power would admit to

such a significant weakness. I can't decide if it's part of your charm or if you're foolish."

I snorted. "That'd be my stupidity. But don't mistake that for an easy mark. The last bitch that tried died a painful death."

Sullivan threw his head back and laughed. "I like you."

"So does the son of Hades," Tsekani interjected.

The alpha's laughter cut off abruptly. "You keep interesting company. I would be honored to help provide a cage for the shifter. I will also come over tomorrow night and see what I can do about the feral."

I pushed off the cushion and stood up like I was in the same shape as Nana. "I would appreciate all the help you can give me. As you can tell, I'm swimming in the dark."

Tsekani shook the alpha's hand. "But you know all about Made shifters." There was a snarl in his voice. He must have sensed the truth of Tsekani through their connection.

I shrugged my shoulders. "Nothing about how to make them. I killed the Tainted witch that made Tsekani and Layla. And I wish I could do it again and make her suffer more."

Sullivan smiled and clapped my shoulder. "I'm glad I don't have to reassess my decision about helping you. Let's get the cage loaded into your truck."

He'd definitely picked up that Tsekani was made. Good to know. I would have led with that if I'd known. In his shoes, I would want to strangle anyone willing to twist a creature into something unnatural for their DNA. No one deserved to be forced into the situation.

I knew Layla and Tsekani were both happy. However, I also knew they were angry over the way Myrna took them as babies and magically forced their bodies to merge with the animals she selected. I couldn't imagine anything worse than having that choice made for me before I was able to do much beyond cry, eat, and sleep.

* * *

"I'M REMOVING the sleep spell. Back away from the cage, Phoebe. You don't want to be that close when he wakes up."

I moved so fast I created enough wind to blow my hair around a little. Nana cackled and pointed at me. "That got her doing the Black-Friday-Mall-Walk. I thought only old ladies like me did that." I rolled my eyes at my grandmother. "There is only one crockpot left at eighty percent off. Will she get it before someone else?" She modified the pitch of her voice, so she sounded like a TV announcer.

Nina snort-laughed, and my mom joined her. A thump from the stairs was followed by Layla's curse and laughter. "You'd be moving even faster if you'd heard the stories that I did an hour ago. Why are you still awake anyway? It's almost eleven at night."

Nana wiped tears from her cheeks as her laughter subsided. "Magical people are night owls. They've got our schedules all screwed up."

"You're right." I turned to my daughter. "You can watch the show, then it's time for bed. You have school early in the morning."

It had taken Tsekani and Brody quite a bit of maneuvering to get the cage downstairs and into the storage room off of my magical kitchen. I bumped into the table holding the half-finished seal and watched through the two open doors.

One second the shifter was asleep, and the next, he jumped to his feet and had his hands wrapped around the bars. He didn't seem to notice the smoke that drifted off his flesh where he clenched the metal.

He was too busy snarling and lunging at the front of the cage. His gaze landed on me, and his attempts to get free increased. Claws raked the air as he reached through the bars.

"I can't get a good read on his signature to see if he is under a compulsion or not. His energy is too chaotic and frenetic."

Tsekani nodded his head with a furrowed brow. "All I sense is chaos from him."

"And blood lust," Layla called out as she made it down to the basement. She was moving slowly, but she was walking on her own.

"Sweeeeet." The feral was keening and had stopped fighting to get to me. His hands were bloody, blistered messes as he reached through toward Layla.

She stopped and growled, baring her teeth at him. He hit the bars with his chest and snarled at her. His canines were massive when he curled his upper lip. Brody stepped in between Layla and the feral. "You need to go back upstairs. You're too close to your heat cycle and are driving him nuts. He's pissed enough as it is."

"Dammit. I just got down the stairs. Help me back up, Phoebe. I want to hear all about the cute alpha that was flirting with you."

Nana got off her chair and hurried to Layla. "I want to hear this, too. Although, I don't imagine Aidoneus will like her seeing anyone else. Two gorgeous guys fighting over her would be fun to watch."

"Who's doing the Black-Friday-Mall-Walk now?" I snorted and wrapped an arm around Layla's shoulders as we climbed up after Nana. "I admit Sullivan is cute, but he did nothing for me. And he backed off when Tsekani mentioned the son of Hades, so I don't' think he was all that interested in me, either. I want to see his reaction to you when he comes tomorrow night."

"Oh! Ask him to help you through your heat cycle, Layla."

"Nana!" I couldn't believe what she was suggesting. I

could never be so casual about sex. Then again, my heart lived in my vagina, so I shouldn't be surprised.

"What? It's painful for her if she doesn't have a man service her. No woman should go through that."

"What happens with shifter women that prefer women for their partners?" We all looked up to see Selene, our resident ghoul standing in the kitchen, holding a rib in one hand. "Does sex with a woman help their pain?"

Layla shook her head. "Not at all. There's something in semen that does the trick. Nature's way of keeping the species going."

"Well, someone should have had a conversation with Mother Nature," my mom called out from behind us. "Women shouldn't be forced to have to be with a man if they don't want to."

This was the weirdest location to discuss sex and shifter heat cycles and how women suffered. I nodded my head in agreement, rolling with the crazy. It was easier than asking them to wait until we could see each other while we talked.

CHAPTER 13

"*A*re you sure this is a good idea? It feels like too big of a risk to drive her around the area," I said, pointing at the ghoul standing next to Layla.

Tarja flicked her tail rapidly while her annoyance came through our bond loud and clear. "*It's our best shot at trying to locate the Tainted that created her. It might be Zaleria. If it's not, we need to stop whoever did create her. And, now that you are fully invested in your magic, you should be able to pick up the remnants of resurrection magic. As you discovered from Fiona, it's not always malicious in intent, but death always lingers nearby.*"

I sucked in a deep breath and ignored the exhaustion weighing me down. It was a long night listening to the feral howl until Nana ordered me to put a spell around the room where the cage was, so she could sleep.

There was nothing more I could do about the shifter in the basement, so I decided to focus on the other case on my plate at the moment. Selene deserved to have a safe new ghoul life or a peaceful rest in the afterlife.

"Alright. I've got this. Let's head out. If there are any problems with the shifter, call me right away." I felt Tarja's approval through our link. I'd swear she was smiling as she walked up the porch steps to the open front door.

Layla walked to the driver's side door. "I'll drive. That way, you can focus on your magic."

I climbed into the passenger side. "Sounds good to me. Let's grab a coffee on our way. I'm ready to fall asleep."

Selene buckled up in the middle of the back seat. "Thank you for helping me. I know you have a lot on your plate. Not to mention that you haven't slept more than four or five hours a night since I arrived, and last night was even worse."

I reached back and squeezed her hand. "It's my job. Besides, I could never ignore what was done to you. No one should force such an existence on another."

"Even though you didn't ask for this, you can have a happy life. Don't give up hope for that possibility. It's not easy to let go of the anger and frustration, but you have to if you want any chance at a better life. Otherwise, you will be a bitter ghoul with no friends, and then you'd be living up to the mundie vision of your kind. You deserve more than that." There were no outward signs that Layla's words came from experience.

She'd lived through something horrific when she was a baby, and I had no doubt she remembered every moment. And, I doubted her pain ended when she was turned. She had years of agony learning how to be a shifter and adjust to life with an animal half.

Selene sighed, and I turned away to give her a semblance of privacy when I noticed the sheen in her eyes. "I'm not sure how to let all of this anger go. I'm so angry over being killed then brought back as this abomination. I feel how wrong I am."

"You aren't a monstrosity. My best friend made her grandmother a ghoul by accident. She isn't Tainted, and her grandmother has been an integral part of her life and helping her fight evil. From what I've read, you feel that way because you don't have your soul," I reassured her.

Selene needed to know she could do good with the hand she'd been dealt. Many were given a raw deal, but that didn't mean there was nothing they could do. I'd seen cancer patients that were given weeks to live use their last days to ensure rescued animals had homes. Or foster children had gifts to open Christmas morning.

"We will figure this out, and I will find a place for you within my company, so you won't have to worry about how you will survive."

Selene sniffed in the backseat. "Why are you helping me? You could have sent me away."

"I couldn't live with myself if I didn't help you. I've been given this gift that I can hardly comprehend most days. Not to mention all this money and a company that's constantly making more. I was built to help others. That's why I was a nurse for twenty years. I can't imagine not doing it. Eventually, I hope to do more."

"You will do great things. I just know it. There are so many in the magical world that need help in one way or another. I know numerous shifters that don't have enough control over their animals to hold down a job, so they and their families live in poverty," Layla replied.

"Witches, too. Most kids can't attend school because they cause fires or flood bathrooms, so one parent has to stay home and take care of them," Selene added. "My mom stayed home with me, and we had to live off government aid after my dad abandoned us. There are countless families out there that need help."

My heart clenched. There was no way I could solve all the world's problems, but I was damn sure going to help those in my territory. "Sounds like I better start making a to-do list.

In fact, Selene, you can do that for me. Coffee. Yes! I'd like a chocolate croissant, too."

"Can I get a sausage biscuit? And, pumpkin latte?"

I turned to grimace at Selene. "You're one of those girls?"

She laughed. "What girls?"

"What Fiona and I used to call the Fall Spice Girls. They go gaga over the shit the second it comes out and consume gallons of every drink, particularly the pumpkin spice ones. Treats, too," I explained while Layla placed our order and drove forward.

Selene laughed and shrugged. "I used to love pumpkin. It might be different now. My tastes have changed drastically."

"Just because you went from being a vegan to a mostly meat diet doesn't mean what you like will change. Tell me more about what you remember when you escaped."

Layla pulled up to the window and distributed our drinks and treats while Selene thought about what she could recall. I'd devoured half of my croissant by the time she started talking.

"I remember waves and houses. Nothing stands out for me until I got to the main road and felt safe to decide where to go. Like I told you before, I knew I was wrong and didn't trust myself around anyone, so I stuck to the woods."

I sipped my highly caffeinated drink and wanted to moan. I needed the boost. "Given that you walked for days to reach me, let's drive through town slowly, then head to Lincolnville along the north coast. I don't think we will find anything here in Camden, but I don't want to rule it out entirely."

"I agree with you. She's not in this town," Selene said around a mouthful. I rolled the windows down as Layla drove leisurely through the streets. "I wouldn't stay in a place the Pleiades might come across me. In fact, I wouldn't remain in the same state as you."

I put my head out the window for a second, allowing the

wind to cool the hot flash that started in my feet and climbed throughout my body. I thought I was years away from having them. They sucked beyond anything I could imagine. My energy was zapped thanks to the Hellmouth, and now I was sweating like a pig, and I was only in my early forties.

"Why wouldn't you want to be close to me?" I assumed witches would be vying for a position close to me. They all coveted my power. Seemed like they'd stalk me, looking for my weaknesses and a way to convince me to give them my powers.

Layla snorted and shot me a look that screamed, 'are you daft, woman?' "If they're encroaching on Dark magic, they would want to be far away from the one being that would make them pay. I've never heard of anyone making a ghoul by accident like Fiona."

"Neither have I," Selene added. "The thought of having our powers stripped, or worse, keeps most witches from giving into temptation and flirting with the Dark side."

"What? I can't strip someone of their power, can I?" The idea was violent and went against the oath I took as a nurse.

But that's not who you are anymore. No, it wasn't. The world I lived in wasn't fluffy and friendly. It was cutthroat and violent. But beautiful and full of possibility at the same time.

Layla tsked me. "Of course you can. Hattie did it several times when witches Turned. It was that or kill them. She preferred to leave them powerless. She thought it taught them a lesson about greed."

What was one more responsibility to add to my list? It was admittedly long, but with the friends and family I had behind me, it wasn't more than I could handle. Or, maybe it was. The Hellmouth was taking more out of me than Aidoneus had anticipated. I'd have to check in with him and see if it was the same for him.

"Well, let's find this one so I can practice."

"With pleasure," Layla said, then turned down the street leading to Marilee's Bakery. Mmmm. We should have gone there for coffee. She made a mean tart. Her cookies were delicious, as well.

I focused on the magic surrounding us as we drove. There were so many threads coming at me, I got dizzy within seconds. *Sort through the feedback like Tarja told you.* Easier said than done. But not impossible. I had to remember that.

Closing my eyes, I focused on the familiar witchy magic. The earthy Fae power, followed by the shifters, vampires, and other paranormals. My eyes snapped open. There were Dark threads throughout town. I couldn't tell if they were recent or from Myrna.

It was too much to hold onto, so I let them go. "Let's head to the Lincolnville-Rockland area. I think checking the towns in that direction first is the best idea."

Selene babbled as we drove while I practiced distinguishing magical signatures. They permeated the area, so they followed us as Layla drove. It was harder to unwind them and identify the various species. I thought I could locate witches and Fae with few problems by the time we reached Rockland.

Layla parked, and we got out. We were on the edge of the main strip where touristy shops were located. This was a bigger area than Lincolnville but an excellent place to start. Selene was shaking when I turned to ask her which direction.

I clasped her hands. "What's wrong? Is it too much for you?"

She started to shake her head then stopped. "Honestly, I'm terrified. There are so many people down there. The cravings never really leave me, and I am so afraid I will start gnawing on someone's arm before I know what I'm doing."

I kept my shock in check and didn't let my eyes widen.

My heart made up for that by hammering triple time. "You have never once looked at any of us sideways. Why do you think you will attack now?"

She shrugged her shoulders but followed when I started walking. I hoped she wouldn't notice we were moving. "I eat all the time because I don't want the cravings to get the better of me. Maybe that's why I haven't done anything yet."

Layla scoffed and stepped in next to us on the sidewalk, so we both flanked Selene. "You can relax. You haven't been starving yourself. From what I read, that's the only time ghouls tend to attack and eat mundies. We can stop and get you a burger, but I'm certain you're going to be alright. The real question is if you think people will recognize you in this area. You're supposed to be dead, after all."

Selene took a deep breath and lifted her chin. Layla's reassurance seemed to prove to her she was going to be alright. "I doubt anyone I know will be here. I grew up in Salem. My family managed to evade the witch trials in the sixteen-hundreds and refused to leave after that. My grandma used to tell me that I couldn't let them drive me away. I'm not sure who she thought was trying to force us out. The witch hunts stopped so long ago, it's hardly remembered by most."

I had never considered what that time in history must have been like for witches. They had to be scared out of their minds. I understand why they wanted to stay secret. Mundies wouldn't handle the news well.

"Is anything familiar in the area?" I asked as we turned down the main drag.

"Can I get a cheeseburger? Just in case?" Selene asked when a burger joint came into view.

"Sure," I agreed. I could use the break. I was freaking exhausted. It might not be possible for me to remain connected to the Hellmouth if this continued. We hadn't been walking for five minutes, and I wanted a break.

I handed Selene some cash and sat at a table outside while she and Layla went inside and ordered some food. My senses tingled, and the wind brought the smell of freesia flowers. There was a Fae close by. I scanned the crowd inside the restaurant then outside. I might be able to detect their magic, but I couldn't identify them.

I got up and walked to the edge of the building to glance around the area. Then, I saw a brown-skinned woman dancing close to a large oak tree down the street behind us. She was tall and willowy and could double as a life-sized paper doll. She was so skinny. Those pointed ears left no doubt she was Fae.

I was surprised she was in public and held my breath while a couple walked within a foot of her. They never so much as glanced in her direction. They couldn't see her. Good to know. I watched as she held her arms out at her sides and spun in a circle.

"Phoebe! We've got trouble."

I spun around when I heard Layla's frantic voice. She was running in the opposite direction. Adrenaline dumped into my system and fueled my flight after her. Selene was so far ahead of us, I wondered how ghouls could move that quick.

"What happened?"

Layla turned her head. Her lips were pursed, and her eyes narrowed. "We were standing in line when she just took off."

Selene turned left, and we lost sight of her. I put on a burst of speed, catching up with Layla. She wasn't moving as fast as she usually would because she was still healing from her injuries. The two of us weren't the best choice for this mission.

I got a stitch in my side as we ran past houses. A little girl stopped jumping rope and watched us pass. We turned left and didn't see Selene anywhere. "Do you smell where she went?"

Laughter echoed from a house partway down the block. Layla tapped her nose into the air and nodded. "This way."

I followed behind her and scanned the yards as we went. We reached the sixth house, and Layla cut into one of the yards. "She's back here."

We slowed our approach and tiptoed to the backyard. Two women were sitting at a patio table talking. Selene walked toward the table with sure steps. A snarl left her and stopped the conversation. "What the hell?"

Selene launched herself into the air. Cursing, I ran to stop her. Layla ran past me and jumped on her, knocking her to the ground. Selene growled and snapped her teeth at Layla. "What's your problem? We were about to get your hamburger. You can't go around attacking people."

Selene bucked and jolted, trying to throw Layla off her. The women stopped screaming and jumped from the table. "What's going on? Why are her eyes red?"

The other woman sobbed. "She was going to kill us!"

I held out my hands. "It's alright. Nothing is going to happen to you guys. You alright, Layla?"

"I could be better."

The women were staring at us with wide eyes. I needed them to stay there until I figured out what to do. I concentrated on my desire to keep them in place. "Custodia." The mundies stiffened and went glassy-eyed.

Satisfied they weren't going to take off and call the cops, I focused on Selene. My heart broke for the ghoul. She would never forgive herself if she hurt anyone. I needed her to stop fighting Layla, so we could get her back to my house. "*Catenas ligant magicis.*"

Silver chains made of light surrounded Selene and Layla, who jumped off before they bound them together. Selene lifted her torso off the ground but didn't make it any further as the magic bound her. She wiggled and grunted, then snarled at me, snapping her teeth.

"What the hell happened?"

"I have no idea, but I'm going to contact Tarja and ask how to handle this." I focused on my familiar *"Tarja?"*

"What is it, Phoebe? Is everything alright? Did you find the witch?"

I glanced at Selene, who was trying to bite and dislodge Layla. The shifter draped her body over her back. *"No. Something happened to Selene. She was afraid of attacking someone, so we stopped to get her a burger, and she freaked out. After a short chase, we caught her about to attack two mundies in their backyard. She's snapping at Layla, and her eyes are red."*

"Shit. She's been possessed by a demon. How did you miss that?"

I bristled at the accusation, but I did think of the moment in Camden when I was overwhelmed by the various magics. I'd even sensed Dark energy. Could that have been when the demon got to her?

"What exactly are you saying? I didn't miss anything. We were in the car until twenty minutes ago, so there was no opportunity for her to be possessed. How do I erase the mundies' memories? I wrapped her in magical chains."

"I'm sorry. I wasn't implying you did anything wrong. I wanted to know how demons entered Camden without alerting you and Aidoneus. Bring her home, and we can get to the bottom of this," Tarja said apologetically.

"Go get the car," I told Layla. She nodded her head and took off. *"What do I do about the mundies?"*

"Call Lilith and tell her to bring a potion to erase the last half hour from these women. The potions don't work under most circumstances, but they weren't injured, and it hasn't been that long."

"Will do. See you soon." I pulled the cell from my back pocket and dialed Lilith.

"What can I do for you, Phoebe?"

"I need you to bring a potion to erase the memory of two mundies."

Lilith's gasp carried a hint of an accusation. "Where? What happened?"

I gave her the address and told her what happened with Selene, then advised she bring Bridget or Clio and be fast about it. I had no desire to wait here any longer than I had to besides the fact that I had no explanation if they got any visitors.

Selene's cursing and growling were going to attract attention. *"Magicae ioculatio."* I loved my powers. There were many times I could have used magical duct tape when I was arguing with Miles.

CHAPTER 14

"What's wrong, Queenie?" Aidoneus's voice settled my stomach. I had no idea if it was the timber or his magic, but I wasn't going to question it.

Lilith had arrived with the potion within fifteen minutes, and Layla was driving us back to my house. I realized I had no idea what to do with Selene once we got home. "Selene has been possessed, and I have no idea what to do with her, so I am going to need your help."

"How did that happen? I didn't sense any demons crossing over. Where is she now?" I tried not to take the snarl in his voice as an accusation.

I clenched my jaw and spoke through gritted teeth. "We were out trying to find the witch that created her when we stopped to get her a burger. She was fine one second and not the next. Layla and I stopped her before she could attack anyone, and now I have her contained. We'll meet you back at my house if you can pull yourself away from the Hellmouth."

"Phoebe..." I hung up the phone before he could continue what he was going to say.

Layla glanced in the rearview mirror. "What do you think is going to happen to her? We aren't going to have to kill her, are we?"

I rubbed the ache in my chest. "Honestly, I have no idea. As you know, there isn't much information beyond their risk and how to kill them. The magical world should have an app where we can go to get answers. It's dangerous not having information readily available. Why keep it secret?"

Layla chuckled, but the sound held no mirth. "Witches are proprietary creatures. And they don't want to help anyone else get powerful. They don't want a potential enemy they can't beat. Besides, each family keeps their own grimoires, and those are magically bound to their family line. That's sacred."

"I get your point. I don't want anyone outside the family looking at the grimoire Hattie gave me, and it doesn't contain information passed down from my ancestors."

"No, but it will. You can remedy the lack of information for Nina and those that follow. Once we discover the information about how to help Selene, you can add it to the book. You can also add information about how to handle the Hellmouth. You've got dark circles, so I can only imagine they'll need to balance the magic it takes."

"That's another thing I'm going to have to ask Aidoneus about. He said it wouldn't take so much." My stomach fluttered as Layla turned down the long driveway leading to the house.

Magic tingled up and down my spine then spread through my limbs as soon as we crossed my ward. It recognized me with a warmth that welcomed me home. It was the best part of returning any time I left.

This time there was another sensation deeper in my gut that pulsed with the power of the stars. It tied me to the Earth. I could feel the darker energy pulsing against the other side. That had to be the Hellmouth. I felt the barest trickle of power heading that direction. That was a false representation of what it actually took from me.

"Speaking of, he doesn't seem too happy to see us," Layla observed as she pulled up in the roundabout in front of the house.

My gaze flicked to Aidoneus standing on the porch. "He probably didn't like me hanging up."

Layla parked the car, and I got out then opened the back door. Aidoneus was at my side before I could lean in and try to get Selene out. His heat was a live wire on my left side.

"I've got her," he offered and latched onto her ankles, then dragged her out of the vehicle before he picked her up. She snarled at him and tried to bite him. He didn't say a word, just placed a finger to her forehead. She slumped in his arms, and he turned and climbed the porch stairs.

I hurried behind him and opened the front door. "Mom, Nana, Thia, we're back. Selene has been possessed, so stay back, okay?"

Tarja and my mom walked in from the kitchen, and I waved her back. "Stay in the kitchen. I think we're going to contain her downstairs."

"Is she alright?" My mom wrung a dish towel between her hands.

I embraced her and urged her back inside the kitchen in time to see Nana sitting on her stool. I gave her a side hug. "I'm not sure. I have no idea what happened, but a demon got a hold of her."

Aidoneus paused by the door to the basement and set Selene on the ground in the pantry. "A chaos demon possessed her. It's a higher-level. This one didn't come through the Hellmouth. It's been here a while, but I can't say how long."

"How did it get inside her?" Nana asked.

"And, how do we get it out?" I added as I grabbed a glass of iced tea.

"A demon that powerful can possess a ghoul without even trying because there is no soul to overcome. Otherwise, they would need permission from the person. A soul has natural protections that prevent anything from taking over."

"You aren't going to like how we get chaos out of her." Aidoneus pinned me with a stare that held compassion. My stomach roiled as I saw how sorry he felt for me. "The only way to get it out is to kill Selene."

Yep, it was as bad as I thought. "There is no way we are killing her. She deserves a chance at life. Someone took her life then a witch brought her back to use her. I promised her I would help her. You need to find me another answer."

"Can't you just make it leave her? You're a god of the Underworld, right?" Go, mom. That was a great point.

Aidoneus's sigh wasn't reassuring. "It doesn't work that way. The demon is clinging to her body, and the only way I can break his hold is to slice through her insides which will kill her."

"I need to think on this. There is a way, and I am going to find it. In the meantime, we need to contain her. Will the cage hold her?"

"The cage is magically reinforced steel. It will hold. But there is a feral shifter inside it at the moment."

That's right. I had another problem to deal with. "The alpha will be here soon." Tarja put the shifter back to sleep. "Tsekani, get him outside, then Aidoneus can place Selene inside and secure her."

I turned away from the group to get a cup of coffee. My head was throbbing, and my body ached with a level of fatigue I'd never felt before. Not even after a grueling forty-eight-hour shift at the hospital. I needed to figure out how to balance my magical life with my energy reserves.

I didn't know if it was a life spent as a mundie that was causing me all sorts of problems or if it was the addition of the Hellmouth or the ghoul or the feral shifter. Laying it all out like that settled the concern raging in the background. It wasn't that I was somehow incapable, or less than.

* * *

SULLIVAN WALKED toward me with swagger and heat. His power was unmistakable and a draw for anyone with eyeballs. I'd bet a combination of that and his good looks had men and women alike fawning all over him. He was attractive. I'd give him that.

The two guys flanking him were his muscle. I'd met Mike and Dave when I was at the compound before, and they were just as frightening on my property.

"Sullivan. Thank you for coming. My familiar still has the shifter under a sleep spell."

The alpha didn't stop until he reached me and lifted my hand to his mouth, where he kissed the back of it. It made my cheeks flush. "Right to work, I see. I prefer to enjoy a beautiful woman before I get down to business." I got lost in Sullivan's amber eyes for a second when a flare of rage pulsed through my body.

Pulling my hand from his, I stepped back and tried to determine where it was coming from. It wasn't Layla or Tsekani. Thia fluttered around the backyard, positioning pixies around the yard, so I doubted it was her.

My gaze landed on Aidon coming out of the house. His eyes glowed red and were narrowed on the alpha. My insides did a little flip at the thought of him caring about me so much that he would be jealous and territorial.

After what I went through with Miles, I had planned on remaining single for a long time. *That one is worth breaking that vow to yourself. He's nothing like that dirtbag that never appreciated you.*

"That's flattering, but not necessary. I'm busy and find myself with another crisis on my hands. I'd like to help this poor shifter if I can before I move onto the latest problem."

Sullivan turned to the side with a nod of his head. His entire being changed. Gone was the sensual element to his bearing. He was all business, and his power increased in the air around us. It had sharp claws that promised to make marks across my throat if I crossed him.

He must have sensed the son of Hades was near and responded to the nonverbal cue Aidoneus had sent out.

My gut told me Aidoneus would win in a fight. Having just gotten a peek at Sully's true power for the first time since I met him, I knew he'd give Aidon a run for his money. "Sullivan, this is Aidoneus, son of Hades and agent of the Underworld Investigative Services. Aidon, this is Sully, the Alpha of the Grey Crest pack. He's here to help with the feral shifter."

"Good to meet you," Aidoneus said as he stopped beside me and crossed his arms over his chest.

"The pleasure is all mine. I've never encountered a UIS agent. Or one of your kind. Your magic is...not what I expected." Sullivan's pause was likely because he didn't know how to interpret what he was sensing.

The Hellmouth had shifted the feel of magic surrounding my property. Mythia was the first to tell me the pixies were unsettled, but were proud to be part of a historic team. Layla told me the shifters felt the same. Apparently, it took someone with great power and bravery to agree to create and police a Hellmouth. The pixies saw it as the equivalent to the portal between realms my best friend Fiona guarded.

"That's because Aidoneus and I created a Hellmouth to control the demons that can cross the veil from the Underworld. It is tied to the two of us and our magic. Apparently, that has seeped into my land and altered the signature."

Sullivan's eyes widened before his gaze shuttered, hiding his discomfort. "I wasn't informed about this." His anger over that fact came through loud and clear.

Should I have notified him? Or any of the other powerful magical people in the area? *"Tarja? Was I expected to notify him I was opening a Hellmouth?"*

My familiar was sitting on a low retaining wall a foot from me and turned to face me when I reached out through our link. *"It is seen as respectful to inform others about events that may impact them. In this case, I did not deem this as necessary to share. It would have brought many unnecessary objections and distract you from the task at hand. He has no reason to be offended. You have taken steps to keep demons out of our realm, and the magic is contained to yours and Aindoneus properties."*

I wasn't sure I agreed entirely with her, but I understood her reasoning. The thought of having such a dangerous portal close by would no doubt strike fear in everyone. However, we did not intend to use it to make it easier for demons to enter our world.

I lifted my chin in the air. "There was no need. This doesn't impact you or your shifters. The Hellmouth was created to keep demons out and make it nearly impossible for Tainted witches to summon them to do their bidding. That's not why I called you here. This feral shifter needs help. Can you assist, or not?"

Sullivan narrowed his eyes at me. I felt his power try to force me to submit. It was easily ignored. He shook his head when I merely lifted one eyebrow at him. I might have made an enemy of him. Still, I refused to back down, and I refused to get his permission before taking steps to protect everyone from demons in my territory.

"The feral shifter is trying to fight my sleep spell," Tarja interjected, breaking the stare-down.

I turned away and approached the shifter that was writhing on the ground with his eyes closed. Sullivan stopped right next to me and glanced down at the guy. I must not have upset him too badly.

"His energy is foul. He might be too far gone. Can you lift the sleep spell? Mike, Dave, hold him down." The two shifters knelt next to the feral. I hadn't noticed where they were standing before that moment. The thought was unnerving. I should have been more aware of those two being so close to me.

Snarling and snapping teeth told me the second Tarja lifted her spell. Muscles bulged on the two guys holding the feral down. He was stronger than them, and I worried he would get free. I looked over and checked where my daughter, Nana, and mom were standing. The last thing I wanted was for them to be hurt.

They were between Layla and Tsekani. I bet they positioned themselves there on purpose. Everyone knew how important their safety was to me. And they wouldn't let anything happen to my family.

Sullivan knelt next to the Feral's head and placed his hand on the guy's forehead. The feral snapped and tried to bite him, but Sully ignored it and locked gazes with the shifter.

"Shift." Sullivan's command was growled and accompanied by an intense rush of power that made me want to comply, even though I wasn't a shifter.

The feral continued to snarl and snap at Sullivan. A shiver went down my body when Sullivan reissued the command. It seemed to aggravate the shifter being held down even more.

The feral bucked, and one of Sullivan's shifters, I wasn't sure if to was Mike or Dave, lost his hold. The feral's teeth were embedded in Sully's forearm before anyone could say anything. Sullivan punched the feral in the side of the skull, breaking the skin and making him bleed. The blow didn't faze the shifter in the slightest.

He continued to snap at those around him. I took a step forward, but Aidoneus shook his head and urged me to back away. Doing nothing didn't sit well with me, but ultimately, I had no idea what I could do to help with the situation.

The shifter that had been dislodged was pissed and landed on top of the feral before he dug his claws into his side. It subdued the feral a degree, and Sullivan locked gazes with him again.

For the third time, Sullivan tried to command him to shift. Once again, it angered the feral and made it react with more aggression. He was more powerful than the two, but Sully was prepared this time and had held the feral's shoulders, so he wasn't able to move.

This wasn't going to work. I didn't want him asleep, but I needed to do something to figure this situation out. I pictured the feral surrounded by a clear cage without including Sullivan, Mike, or Dave. I had no idea how long I could hold a containment spell like this or if it would work, but I needed to try.

"Layla, Tseki, watch my family." I replayed the image I wanted in my mind to keep my intent clear. "*Contineo.*"

I felt the spell leave me but wasn't sure it actually worked. I hesitated to take the chance with my family so close. I took a deep breath for resolve. "Let him go. He should be contained. But, be ready to jump on him if my spell didn't work."

Realizing what I'd done, Layla and Tseki moved in front of my mom and Nana. Nina was young and could take off to the house. Aidoneus wrapped an arm around me, and I felt his desire to shove me behind his back. The fact that he didn't tell me he trusted my magic. I was touched. Especially since I wasn't sure it was warranted.

Sullivan and his shifters jumped to their feet and took a couple steps backward. The feral was on his feet a second later and snarling at us. He lunged toward Sullivan, trying to attack him. An invisible wall stopped him.

I blew out a breath and nodded in satisfaction. Sullivan ran a hand through his hair and met my gaze. "That shifter's mind is a jumbled mess. There are no coherent thoughts that I could pick up on. When they're too far gone to obey an alpha's commands, we only have one choice."

My stomach flipped, and a boulder settled there, making me sick. "What's that?" I was certain what he was going to say, and I would never agree.

"I need to kill him before he gets loose and hurts innocents. He will not hesitate to kill women and children that get in his way. There's no choice."

I shook my head vigorously. "There is always a choice. I will not let him be killed. Especially when I can feel magic surrounding him."

"I feel it too," Sullivan agreed. "I don't like it any more than you do, but no one has ever been able to break such an enchantment."

"Give me a moment. I need to think and consult with my familiar. Can you hang around for a bit?"

Sullivan nodded, and I crossed and took a seat next to Tarja. The weight of the situation was heavy on my shoulders, making it difficult to breathe. *Put on your big girl panties and find a solution to this problem. Everyone believes in you, but you. Time to change that, Pheebs.*

CHAPTER 15

"I'm here," Stella announced as she rushed through the back door. I twisted from my spot next to Tarja on the retaining wall. "I can see I've missed a lot. How can I help?"

Giving my childhood best friend magic had been an accident, but it was the best mistake I'd ever made. Stella was eager and willing to jump in with both feet, no questions asked. It made learning magic and this journey fun and less of a chore. With her at my side, solving all of these problems didn't seem like such a burden.

"I'm about to deal with this feral shifter. How can I break this enchantment on the feral? We have to save him, Tarja?" I wouldn't accept anything less.

I might think like a mundie and need to adjust to how things worked in the magical world, but there was only so far that I was willing to go. I'd be damned if this world made me cold and callous. Those closest to me would adjust how they thought, as well.

Stella shivered and crossed her arms over her chest.

"That's one big wolf. He doesn't feel right. And, he's pissed at you, Pheebs."

My familiar walked toward the snarling shifter. *"You will need to cast a circle and call on the elements. Simple chants cannot break through this much power."*

"Oooh. Do we get to do a *witchual*?" Stella clapped her hands and jumped, then paused as her gaze landed on Sullivan for the first time.

I got to my feet and joined her with a smile on my face. Her joy was contagious. *"Witchual?"* I lifted one eyebrow, making her shrug. I supposed it fit, even if it didn't sound like what any witch I'd met would say. "This is Sullivan, the alpha of the local Grey Crest pack. He came to try and help with the feral shifter. This is Stella, my best friend, and fellow witch."

Sullivan scanned Stella, the appreciation in his gaze evident. He lifted her hand and kissed the back of it. "Pleased to make your acquaintance, Stella."

"Boy, you pack a powerful punch, don't you? Not as much oomph as Aidoneus here, but there's no ignoring you." Stella observed, unaffected by Sully's flirtation.

I cleared my throat and focused on Tarja, wanting to get back on track and avoid a pissing match between Sullivan and Aidoneus. "Alright, casting a circle means I need salt and herbs, right? And candles?"

"We've got it, mom." Nina and Thia exited the house with their arms full. Thia carried a brown ceramic jar with herbs painted on it in green, while Nina had candles and a clear crystal bowl.

Stella joined me as they held them out to us. I grabbed the crystal bowl of salt. Tarja sat next to me. *"Mix the herbs and cast the circle, Phoebe."*

"Can I do the candles at the cardinal points?" Stella asked as she grabbed a candle from Nina.

"Yes, Stella. Light the candles with your witch flames, as Phoebe calls the elements. You recall the ritual you both read about a couple months ago, correct?"

Stella nodded her head up and down rapidly while I struggled to recall the words. I knew the gist of calling the elements. "Is there room for freeform in this? Of course, I know to keep my intent clear to ask the elements to aid in my casting, but do I have to say it word for word?"

"Very few witches can effectively create their own spells, but you have done it from the beginning. Because you know Latin, you've used words you associate with what you want the spell to accomplish. Most aren't what you'd find in most spell books, but for you, it doesn't matter. All that to say, yes, you can likely follow your gut and change the wording."

My chest puffed up, and my head tilted up a fraction higher. "Why didn't you ever tell me this before?"

Tarja's distinct laughter-hack echoed through my mind. *"Because it worked for you, and I didn't want you to get caught up in your head by trying to memorize what wasn't coming naturally for you. If your spells continued to misfire or fail, I would have helped you memorize the spell books."*

"I appreciate you letting me learn in a way that was natural to me. I had no idea I was doing it differently from most, and I am glad I don't care. Step in and help me if I get something wrong here, please." Tarja inclined her head to me in agreement.

I grabbed a handful of herbs from the jar Mythia held and dropped them in the salt. My mom held out my athame, and I stirred the mixture with it. I took several deep breaths while Stella placed the candles five feet from the shifter at each necessary point.

I grabbed a handful of the mixture and started walking in a circle. Stella knelt down and lit the first candle with her pink flames. "Hear me, Guardians of the East, the

Element of Air. We call to you tonight with an open heart and clear voice to ask that you lend your knowledge. Guardians of the South, the Element of Fire we call to thee. We ask for assistance with lighting the passions within so that we may connect more deeply with the world around us."

I paused, hyperaware of Aidoneus's eyes on me as I bent and spread the salt mixture in a circle with the feral at the center. It flash boiled my blood and loosened my body. "Guardians of West, Element of Water. We call you today to lend your emotion and purity to this ritual. Guardians of the North, Powers of Earth, we call to thee and ask that you gift us with your steadfastness and manifestation during this ritual. Enter here and welcome."

Despite the lame finish to my casting, white light burst from the salt circle, and magic surrounded me, making my skin tingle and glow. I held out my hand with the athame and noticed it was bright silver.

The wind picked up, carrying the scent of the fresh ocean with it. The waves crashing against the pebbled shore of my beach grew until mist sprayed us from a hundred yards away in my yard. The candles responded with a column of pink flames three feet high while the ground rumbled gently.

Everyone outside went quiet, even the feral. I stepped closer and held my hands out to him. Stella stepped up and clasped the hand, not holding my ceremonial knife. The feral snapped his teeth and hit the invisible barrier every time he lunged for us.

I felt each impact. Stella steadied me when I jolted initially. I grimaced when blood dribbled from his nose. I was flying blind here. Stella and I had read various other spells in my grimoire, but I couldn't recall any of them specifically.

"What elements do I need to include in this spell?"

143

"You need to unravel the other witch's magic and scatter the remnants of it."

I inclined my head and sucked in a breath while I gathered my thoughts. I knew enough Latin to cast individual minor spells, but not a lengthy sonnet. "Behold this mind, cast adrift and forced to submit; With the power of the elements and the moon in the sky, pull the darkness from him piece by piece and cast it into the flames."

I turned to Stella and nodded. My head throbbed, and sweat covered me from head to toe. Talk about hot flashes. Damn, I should have had more time before they got this bad.

We extended our linked hands behind us, and my purple flames rose, followed by her pink ones. Pink and purple intertwined and wound together. I knew the spell was working when it resembled one of those bug lights that zapped their tiny bodies as they flew into it.

Sparks flew off of our column in a flurry, and the feral dropped to the ground. His eyes fluttered closed, and his jaw shortened, fur receding until brown flesh was left. Next, his claws disappeared and were replaced by normal fingernails. I dropped the invisible containment circle and extinguished my flames when the sparks stopped a second later. We'd done it.

Stella released my hand and reached for the athame. "May I?"

I was happy to let her open the circle. I didn't recall this part of the ceremony. Stella crouched beside the salt mixture. "Thank you for your assistance tonight. It saved a life." She cut through the salt, and wind blew through the circle and out. The pink flames went out, and Tarja jumped over the rim.

"You two make a good team. A witch rarely finds someone to work with so seamlessly. And you broke the enchantment on the feral. He's beginning to stir."

I reacted without thinking and had a barrier up in the blink of an eye. I had no idea what we would face now. Aidoneus's hand was on my back, steadying me. "Can you get him some sweats?" I asked Mythia.

The shifter was far younger than I expected, and I suddenly had no idea what to do. I turned to Sullivan. "I'll follow your lead from here."

He inclined his head and walked forward. "You can lower the barrier."

I swallowed and placed my hand over my racing heart. I didn't like the idea of nothing standing between my mom and Nana when this guy was hanging around. He had been trying to tear our throats out until a moment ago.

Logically, I understood that he was under someone else's spell, but it did little to settle my nerves. It wouldn't take much for the shifter to kill my mom or Nana. Nina might run, but she was my child, and I didn't want her hurt.

I pointed at Sully. "You're responsible for controlling him from here. If he makes a move toward my family, I will not be happy."

One corner of his mouth lifted in a smirk. "You're terrifying. I can sense his wolf now. I won't have any problems ensuring he behaves."

I waved my hand to remove the barrier, only realizing I never spoke when I cast the spell earlier. I had reacted on instinct and out of fear for my family. I wasn't surprised when nothing happened. Someday I would learn how to tap into that level of control.

"*Solvo.*" I dissolved my barrier.

Mythia flew forward and dropped a pair of grey sweats by the shifter. He reached over and slipped them on, then stood up. "I, uh… thank you. I never thought it would end."

Sullivan crossed his arms over his chest. "Who are you?"

The shifter's head snapped from me to Sully before it

instantly lowered. "My name is Zack Chandler." He focused on the ground as he spoke, which was a bit odd.

Sullivan's eyebrows creased. "What happened? Who cast a spell on you, and why? Did a witch attack your pack?"

"I'm going to get the kid something to drink and eat," my mom announced before she headed into the house.

Zack shook his head. "My pack keeps their noses clean. Our alpha never gets involved with other packs or the witches. He prefers not to adopt trouble. I was on a run through our lands when a dark-haired witch threw a spell at me. I couldn't avoid it. The next thing I knew, I was in the dark and being driven by someone else's will."

"Your wolf couldn't fight the commands off? When you release your animal fully, they can often override an enchantment." The shifter didn't react to the snarl in Sully's tone while I wanted to curl into myself and promise I would do better in the future.

Zack pulled the string at the waistband of his pants. "My wolf tried. Countless times. I thought my wolf would truly become feral like the witch accused. You have no idea how hard I fought, Alpha."

My mom came out and held a tray with three sandwiches and a soda out to me. Aidoneus took it and approached the shifter. "Mollie makes the best turkey sandwich in the world. You have to try one. Where are you from?"

Zack picked up a sandwich and bit into it. "I'm from the Silver Paw pack near Portland," he said around a mouthful. His shoulders were no longer at his ears although, his spine was still straight as an arrow. His entire demeanor relaxed as he spoke with Aidoneus.

"What else can you tell us about the witch that did this to you?" Aidoneus held the tray while Zack ate.

I joined them and cracked the can open. "Can you

describe her?" We didn't have a description for Zaleria. She could be standing next to me, and I would never know.

Well, that wasn't entirely true. I would like to think I'd be able to detect her Dark energy. I know some glamours and masks might be able to hide her true nature, but I had a hard time believing it would shield her aura.

Zack ate a couple more bites before he picked up the cola and took a drink. "My mind is fuzzy, and I can't recall all of her details, but I know she has dark hair and light eyes, I think. Her skin is olive-toned. I can't recall what she wore."

"Were her eyes blue or green? Can you remember a color?" C'mon, he had to give me something more.

He tilted his head back and drained the drink, then wiped the back of his hand over his mouth. "Honestly, I can't be sure. I think they were green but really pale. I recall with clarity that my wolf knew right away there was something off with her and tried to run away. She caught me in some kind of tractor beam and pulled me to her."

Stella held up her hand. "Um, is there a counterspell I can cast if I find myself being dragged by a Tainted witch? I don't want to end up under Zaleria's control. Being Phoebe's best friend, I'd pose the highest risk to her safety."

"While Phoebe finishes the seal for the Hellmouth, you need to come and create a charm that will repel magic. It doesn't make you impervious, but it will not allow one to get a grip on you."

Sullivan pursed his lips. "Is this something you can create for shifters? I do not want this witch to do this to one of my wolves."

Stella looped her arm through mine. "We would be happy to provide charms to your pack. Without knowing the process, we cannot give you an estimate of the cost until later. How many will you need?"

"There are three hundred-fifty-seven in my pack right now." I nearly choked when Sullivan told me that. "But if we can start with seventy-two, that will cover my Beta and at least one parent in each family. We can keep the rest close to the packhouse until they are protected."

My heart hammered, and I shot Stella wide, wild eyes. She merely smiled and shifted her focus to Sullivan. "That works for us. We will need a non-refundable deposit to get started. If you're okay with this, you can Venmo me two hundred and fifty dollars."

To my surprise, Sully nodded and pulled his cell from his back pocket. "That works for me. I will pay half as soon as you have an accurate cost per charm, so you can get them made as soon as possible."

"Stella will send you a text letting you know," I told him as he scanned her Venmo code from her phone. "Now, can you help Zack get back to his pack? I have a lot of work ahead of me in the next few days and cannot take time away from that. I have a feeling his mother is worried about him and will want to see him before I can get him back."

Sullivan nodded once. "Shifter mothers are very protective. I know she's worried, and I will be more than happy to help Zack. You two might want to work on an assembly line production to get these charms made. And not just because I want them faster. When Zack tells his pack about what happened and how you can make charms, you'll be getting another order. Word will spread fast."

I nodded my head and turned my back, glaring at Stella. *"Do not panic. I have tried to get Hattie to cooperate with the pixies on providing more charms to the magical world. We will ask Daethie and get the coven involved. It might even be something Nina can help with."*

"I will ask Thicket, but I am finishing the seal before I tackle this project." I hoped finishing that project would alleviate some of the drain on my energy.

CHAPTER 16

"*T*hank you for helping me down here, Aidon. It makes me feel decades younger to watch my Phoebe work." I rolled my eyes at the obvious flirting of my Nana with my boyfriend.

"You don't look like you're a day over sixty," Aidoneus told Nana, making her laugh.

The term didn't seem quite right to me. I had no idea what Aidoneus and I were to each other. Still, neither of us was twenty years young and driven by silly romantic endeavors. I knew the score of situations. Love was a changeable emotion I had yet to experience outside my family.

What Miles and I shared was lust at the beginning that morphed into a roommate situation. At one point, I was certain I loved Miles, but looking back, I saw I was in love with the idea of a partner. Miles saw me as someone to do his errands, clean our house, cook his meals and raise the children. To me, he provided us a comfortable life.

But you never needed him. You worked your ass off and could have done it all by yourself.

Aidoneus and I had only ever operated as partners. He

didn't see me as less than him, and he had every reason to have that belief. He was a freaking powerful god. I watched him help Nana into her seat. She was moving better every day. I had to believe living here and moving around more helped give her youth. I wasn't ready for her to leave us yet.

I motioned to the pixie flying next to Stella. "Thia, can you ask Thicket if he has time to help tonight? I want to finish the seal."

"I've already sent a message. He will be here shortly."

Thank god she seemed to know what I would need before I ever opened my mouth. "Are you sure you aren't a seer?"

The tinkle of bells echoed as Mythia laughed. "I wish. The gift of foresight is rare in Eidothea."

Aidoneus joined us at the table with my project. My stomach turned over, and my heart leaped when he ran his hand over the misshapen metal. "You've made a lot of progress on this. I was surprised to see it when I brought Selene down here earlier."

"She's been working on it a little every day even if she's dealt with crap all day," Stella told him as she went to the wooden boxes on the lower shelves that held the precious metals the pixies had given me. "Phoebe is my idol. I need to adopt some of her work ethic. I'd be a millionaire by now if I did."

I was nervous about continuing the work on this, so I decided to call Fiona and talk to Bas. I had my phone out and was dialing before I checked the time. "Hello," Fiona said in a scratchy voice.

"Crap, Fi! I didn't look at the time. I'll handle this on my own and talk to you later." I pulled the phone from my ear and noticed it was after eight at night in Maine, which meant it was after one in the morning in Cottlehill Wilds.

"No, it's alright. I'm up now, and you know me, I won't

get back to sleep until I know why you called. What's up?" Her voice was bright and eager.

Waking up at the drop of a hat was the curse of being a nurse on overnight shifts. I was the same way. There was a rustling of fabric that told me she had likely sat up in bed.

I chewed my lip, debating for another second. She was willing, so I would ask what she knew without bothering Bas. "I'm working on the seal for the Hellmouth and was curious how Sebastian shapes silver when he works with it. It's too soft to hammer. And I can't force the element to cooperate with me. I really want to get this completed so I can look for a way to get the demon out of Selene."

"Who is it, Butterfly? Does Violet need us?" Sebastian's deep voice sounded like it was right next to the microphone. An image of them sleeping in each other's arms made me flush. I should have thought before I called.

"It's Phoebe. She's working on the seal for the Hellmouth in her area and needs help," she told her boyfriend. "Violet and Thanos are preparing to open the one here. Thanos purchased land near the cliffs where it will be held." Fiona's voice echoed when she spoke again. She had to have put me on speakerphone.

"Do you need me to talk to your fabricator?" Bas asked.

"You're talking to her. I have absolutely no experience with silversmithing, so I am out of my element here. I am trying to force the metal into a three-foot circle that's about six inches thick."

There was more rustling, and then my phone was ringing. I pulled it from my ear and saw they wanted to FaceTime. There was no stopping the way my cheeks heated, or I turned away from my project, so they saw my mom, Nana, and my daughter behind me.

"Good to see you, although you look tired. Don't think I missed the way you slipped the possession of your ghoul in there. We will get back to that." Fiona was dressed in a purple sleep shirt. Her hair was mussed, but she looked like a million bucks. Sebastian had a tight black t-shirt on, and I couldn't help but wonder if he was putting it on a second ago. He seemed like a guy that would sleep naked.

I chuckled my voice warbling and shaking. "You look amazing for being woken up in the middle of the night."

"Hello, Fiona," my mom waved.

Nina got up from the floor and put her face on my shoulder. "Hey, Auntie Fiona. I'm going to help make some charms to protect shifters from being controlled by Tainted and Dark witches."

Fiona's smile widened, showing her joy at seeing Nina. "Wow! You guys have as much going on there as we do here."

"Show me your seal," Sebastian demanded. He was a surly sort. I wondered how he and Fiona got together. Her words had a bite to them at times, but she was always upbeat and happy.

I turned around and cringed when I heard Fiona gasp. I checked to see what she was looking at and found her gaze settled behind me. My stomach dropped to my feet. It was worse than I thought.

Fiona looked down at me a second later. "Is that Aidoneus? We've never actually met before."

"Oh." My cheeks were on fire. I probably looked like a cherry tomato. "Yes, this is Aidoneus, son of Hades and UIS agent stationed here in Camden. He and I opened the Hell-mouth together a few days ago."

Fiona lifted an eyebrow. "And, that's all?"

"Fiona," I growled.

Aidoneus chuckled and placed a hand at the small of my back, letting me know he liked the direction of the conversation. He was always horny. If I didn't know how much he cared about me, I'd worry he was using me to get into my pants. *As if he'd need to. He can crook his finger and get any woman on the planet.*

"It's good to meet the woman Phoebe always talks about. I owe you and your mate thanks for saving her life. Without your gift, Myrna would have killed her months ago, and this world would have been worse for it."

Fiona's eyebrows rose to her hairline while Bas's expression didn't change. "You're right about that. I like to think Fate was behind everything."

"The seal," Sebastian demanded in a growl.

"Yes. Sorry." I handed the phone to Nina, who was still standing close to us. "Hold this and keep it pointed so I can see them, and they can see the seal and me."

Nina nodded her head, and I moved to the side. "This is what I have so far. It needs a lot of work still, so I need to know if you have suggestions for how to get the silver to cooperate with my magical attempts to manipulate it."

Thicket flew down the stairs and stopped on a dime when he caught sight of Fiona and Bas on the phone. He hovered there, gaping at them. "Thicket, this is my friend Fiona and her, uh, mate," I decided I liked the term Aidoneus had used better than boyfriend, "Sebastian. This is Thicket. He's been helping me with this project."

Thicket cleared his throat and bowed to them. "It's a pleasure to meet the Hammer and his Blade."

Fiona's cheeks turned pink, and she shook her head. "You don't have to call us that. My name is Fiona, and this is Sebastian."

"I know your names. Thanks to you, the Fae now have the option of returning to Eidothea without fear of losing our lives to fuel the evil king's corrupt power."

Bas lifted his shoulders. "That would not have been possible without my Blade. She was the power behind the coup." There was no mistaking the pride in his voice then.

"And, you are going to help us with our seal?" Thicket was practically vibrating with excitement.

Bas inclined his head. "I am. You mentioned using magic to shape the metal. That will not work unless you have elemental power. Unless you are part Fae, you do not have that ability, and it will take you ten times longer to get the end result you want."

Thicket's head dropped. "I should have thought of that and told her. They went ahead with the Hellmouth because I assured them it could be done quickly."

"It's difficult to keep in mind the differences between our kinds. But it can still be done quickly. You have witch fire, correct?"

I cast my fire to my hands. That was one thing I could do without a chant easily because it was connected to the core of my being. "Yes, I do. It'll melt it into a puddle, though."

Sebastian shook his head from side to side. "Not if you cast a dampener on the flames. Then you can run your hands over the surface and smooth it out. You've already melted the various pieces together."

Stella crossed to the other side of the table and called her flames. "I'll help. That way, it will go faster."

I glanced down at my hands and watched the flames dancing across my knuckles. I could do this. "*Calor diffundens.*" I decided a more literal approach to create a barrier that would diffuse the heat was best.

Stella repeated the spell, and we lowered our hands a couple inches above the metal. It softened right away, and I was able to use my energy to spread it out. Thicket grabbed a spatula and flew behind us, smoothing the surface as we worked.

I could see progress within seconds. "Oh my God, thank you so much for helping. I've got this from here. I don't want to keep you up any longer."

Bas held up a hand and looked toward Aidon, who was standing in the same place he had been before I went to work on the seal. "Are you etching the runes into the seal? I offered to do it, but Thanos hasn't finished his research on the process yet, so he hasn't told us who will be creating the Hellmouth with him, let alone the details on the seal. I finished the disc, but nothing more."

I continued manipulating the silver while the two guys spoke. The heat built beneath the filter I'd created, and I had to release it before my hands burned up.

Aidoneus ran a hand through his hair. "He is waiting for me. The others, as well. No one else is to proceed until I have confirmed my suspicions about the process. I am compiling the details now and will give it to them. The runes will need to be specific to the pair hosting the Hellmouth. There needs to be a physical representation of the two magical forces coming together."

"Patience isn't my forte. I don't like Fiona and her family being in danger."

Fiona wrapped an arm around Sebastian and laid her head on his chest. "We will wait to hear from Thanos. And, I expect a call soon about your ghoul."

"I will call as soon as I can. Thanks again for the help." Fiona ended the call, and I went back to shaping the seal.

Stella paused and released her filter. "I've been pushing prohibitive energy into the metal. Our purpose is to keep demons in the Underworld, so I figured it couldn't hurt for me to reinforce the metal."

"I've done that every time I work on it. I just forgot to mention it. I wish I'd called him sooner. This is going so fast."

Thicket stopped smoothing and met my gaze. "It is not your failure but mine. I should retire from being the clan smith. I am no longer fit for the role."

I pursed my lips and frowned. "Nonsense. I have nothing

but faith in you. In fact, Stella negotiated a deal with shifters to create charms that will repel magic. We have an order for three hundred and fifty, and we are hoping you will make them while we imbue them with the magic."

"You'll get paid, of course," Stella added.

Tears welled in the little pixie's eyes. "I will not let you down again. I shall start on designs as soon as we are done here."

Aidoneus leaned close to me, his mouth brushing my ear. "You've got a heart of gold, Queenie. That pixie would have lost all purpose in life because of an oversight anyone could have made, and you saved him."

His compliment cracked something in me. He truly saw the heart of who I was and still believed in me. No one had ever had that much faith in me. It made me stand taller. "Thank you. Now, get ready to engrave the runes. We're almost done. Then we can install this on the Hellmouth so you can leave your house to update your people."

Stella and I continued to work for ten more minutes before Thicket declared the seal was ready for engraving. "This will make etching the images easier," Thicket said as he handed what looked like an ice pick to Aidon. "Phoebe, you remain in place and heat the surface, so he can write."

I nodded my head and stayed in place as directed. I waved my hands over a small section. Aidoneus was right behind me, writing on the surface like it was a piece of paper. We did that until two-thirds of the outside was covered in symbols that meant nothing to me.

I didn't need to know what they represented to realize they were a warning and directive. The magic pulsed from the surface, making me fight the urge to flee. I was startled when Nana spoke up. "Mollie, would you help me upstairs?"

"I've got you, Nana," Nina interjected. Apparently, it was

affecting them as well. They left the basement, along with Layla, Mythia, and Thicket.

"Grab Tsekani, Layla. We will need his help hauling this," I called out, then turned to Stella. "You alright?"

She jogged in place and shook her head. "I'm good. I want to see the rest of this. It's the coolest thing I've ever seen."

Aidoneus stepped back when there was only a one-foot diameter in the center that was untouched. "This last symbol will represent the two of us. Your magic and mine. Stella, will you heat the metal while Phoebe and I join hands?"

Stella nodded her head and smoothed her pink flames over the blank space. Aidoneus grabbed my hand, and electricity traveled through me from where our hands touched. I sucked in a breath at the sensual feel of the energy. I didn't expect that.

He held our hands out over the center. I had short arms, and my chest was brushing against the etched surface. There was a battle between the arousal from our connection to the repellant of the seal. "Push our energy into the seal, Queenie."

I closed my eyes and focused on the energy zipping between us, heightening my entire body. "*In urna.*" Lightning burst from our joined hands and struck the metal. Light flared, and the metal began smoking.

We remained in place for a couple minutes before Aidoneus pulled our hands away. I gaped at the intricate knot in the center. It almost looked like two intertwined bodies. There was a symbol on one half that looked like a tribal star and a tribal moon on the other side.

The entire process didn't take that long, but that last part made me want to take Aidoneus home and strip him naked before taking him for a wild ride.

"That was intense," Stella muttered, breaking the moment. Just in time too. I'd hate for Tsekani to walk in on that moment between Aidon and me. He'd know right away what was happening with his shifter nose.

Tsekani bounded down the stairs a few seconds later. "I hope it's ready. I won't be able to stay here for long."

Aidoneus placed a brief kiss on my lips then hefted the seal to the floor. Tsekani clenched his jaw and picked up one side. The guys carried it up the stairs while Stella and I followed. Nana had ice cream when we passed through the kitchen.

"I'm heading home, Pheebs. I can't hold back anymore," Stella said as I headed for the back door.

"I'll call you tomorrow. Thank you for the help. I'm so glad that you're magic is progressing faster than mine, so we could get that done tonight." I didn't check in with my family as I ran to catch up with Aidoneus and Tsekani. I had no desire to traipse around the forest alone in the dark. There were some fears magic couldn't erase entirely.

"You're Herculean. I have no idea how you are handling this so well." I understood Layla's surprise. I was a mess when it came to my magic. Although, I was improving all the time.

I slowed and kept pace with Layla. "I don't think about it. I felt the initial jolt but was able to shove it away. Perhaps it's because I helped create it."

"It's because of our connection," Aidoneus called from several feet ahead of us. "You will be one of the few beings that will be capable of closely monitoring the Hellmouth once this is in place. It will repel everyone else."

We stopped at the site of the Hellmouth, and my heart squeezed. "Why is the groundcover dead? I didn't expect it to infect the foliage like this."

Aidoneus set his end of the seal down on the ground. "Don't set yours down yet," he told Tsekani, then walked to take that end from him. He moved to the right some more, then dropped it into place.

Dust blew up in a cloud, and a low gong sounded as if it had hit something metal underneath the earth. Vibrations shook me and made me lock my knees in place. Aidoneus knelt by the seal and lifted his hand to mine.

"The plants will come back now that there is a seal in place. There was little protection against the malevolent energy flowing from the Underworld. It was caused by the demons trying to push their way free. Come kneel on the other side of the cover. Now we're locking it in place."

The vibrations continued, but the drain on my energy eased back enough that I noticed. I was still exhausted, but I didn't notice it taking so much from me. I situated myself across from Aidoneus and placed my palms on the seal.

I met Aidoneus's sapphire eyes, and he nodded to me. "*Sigillo clausa seris*," I chanted at the same time Aidoneus said something in the foreign language he spoke.

I sank down once I felt the locks click into place. Another task I could check off my growing to-do list. "We did it."

He stood up and picked me up in his arms. "Yes, we did. Let's get you home. You need some rest."

"I can walk," I protested half-heartedly.

He kissed my forehead and kept walking. "I know you can." I sighed and laid my head down, closing my eyes. I'd let him take me home this time. My eyes didn't want to stay open anyway.

CHAPTER 17

$\mathcal{I}$ threw a hand over my eyes to block out the sun blinding me. There was zero desire to get out of bed. Given the height of the sun, I'd bet it was mid-morning. The last thing I remember from the night before was placing the seal on the Hellmouth and Aidoneus carrying me home.

I turned and pulled the covers up to my chin. Staying in the warm, cozy bed sounded perfect. Not having a regular schedule was messing with me in too many ways to count. Silva, Inc. didn't run itself, but Lilith had taken a more prominent role for Hattie when she declined and continued while I got my feet under me.

Unfortunately, my mother had instilled a healthy sense of guilt in me. I couldn't let her do it all. Even though I was woefully unprepared to take on the role of CEO for a major corporation that had its hands in at least five different pies.

"Good morning, Queenie. I brought you some coffee." My eyes snapped open when I heard Aidoneus's deep bass voice.

"You're a pleasant surprise this morning, Yahweh." I covered my mouth with a sheet. Morning breath was not sexy in the least.

He set the tray on the end table next to my bed then sat next to me on the mattress. "I never left. With the Hellmouth finally secured, I decided to take advantage and stay with you."

I sat up against the headboard and grabbed the coffee. The thought of him sleeping next to me comforted and unsettled me at the same time. Miles is the only guy I'd ever spent the entire night with. The dorm wasn't the best place to have overnight guests, so Fiona and I both agreed we would never do that to each other.

"And, you assumed I was alright with you sleeping in my bed?" I arched a brow and sipped the nectar of the gods.

"Don't cover Aidon if you're naked," Nana called out as she entered my room. "I'm just getting something to wear."

I laughed and shook my head. "No one is naked, Nana. We really need to move those clothes into your closet."

She snorted as she walked past me to the massive room called a closet. "These clothes will never fit in mine. We can move things around to make room if you ever want to unpack."

There was room to lend and store my stuff, as well. Seriously, the closet had an island in the center with drawers and shelves on top, plus three sections and a wall of shelving to hold shoes.

"I'll get around to that eventually," I told her with a smile.

My mom entered my room next. If Aidon and I were going to be in a relationship, I would have to inform everyone in the house they couldn't walk in whenever they wanted.

"Good morning, Aidoneus, Phoebe. Sweetheart, I can finish putting your clothes away. They're practically unpacked now, anyway. Every time Mythia does laundry, I hang them up or put them away. I can show you where I put them if you're ever curious."

"You should wear the eggplant jumper," Evanora's voice echoed from the closet. The ghost inserted herself in our daily lives here and there, never being too intrusive.

Aidon and I would never have privacy in this house. I was getting sidetracked by wishful thinking. We weren't officially a couple. I'd cross that bridge when we came to it. "I wondered who was doing my laundry and organizing it. Thanks, mom. I will do the rest right after we get the demon out of Selene." She inclined her head and ducked into the closet.

Aidon's mouth turned down at the edges and his gaze turned in my direction. "I know you want to save her, babe, but I don't see how that is going to be possible without killing her."

"I have some ideas." When we dealt with the feral shifter the night before, and I had to break that enchantment, I got an idea. "I'm going to shower. I will meet you downstairs and fill you in when I'm done."

He cupped my cheek and pressed his lips to mine in a gentle but demanding kiss. Arousal flooded me in an instant and made me forget about having morning breath. I wanted to get my family out of my room then wrap myself around him.

He broke the kiss with a knowing smirk. "See you downstairs."

I climbed off the bed and smacked him on the ass on my way to the bathroom. "How is it that you smell fresh and have on clean clothes?"

Aidon leaned down and nipped the side of my neck. "I'm a god, Phoebe. Procuring clean clothes is an easy one for me. And I showered while you were busy drooling on your pillow."

My face heated, and I lifted my hand to see if there was dried slobber on my chin. That was highly embarrassing. He chuckled and continued out the door. "That man is sex walking," Nana said from far too close.

I jumped and turned to her. "Don't forget dangerous, Nana."

Her head moved up and down. "Yeah, to your underwear. I imagine he's the type that will rip them off your body."

My jaw dropped. I paused next to the shower and gaped at her standing a couple feet away. My mom waited next to her with two outfits draped over her arm. "You've been reading too many romance novels, mom. In reality, men don't rip clothing off of you."

"Maybe not men today, but your father used to tear them from me."

"Mother!" My mom's voice rose an octave, and I understood the sentiment. No one wanted to think of their parents having sex.

I shook my head at my family, although my heart was smiling, then flipped on the shower. I loved my tribe more than I imagined possible. Some of our connections had dimmed while I was married to Miles because I didn't see them often enough.

Ever since I'd come home, I couldn't imagine anything making me live far from them. There was nothing in this world that was worth not having them close to me. My mom and Nana entered the bathroom to change and continued arguing about appropriate conversations. At the same time, I took my sleep shirt off and got under the hot water.

I grabbed my loofah and squirted soap on the sponge. When I scrubbed my body with it, I imagined Aidon using it on his chest and arms, then his legs. I cut those thoughts off. Now was not the time to get lost in a fantasy.

I finished washing my hair, got out, wrapped a towel around my torso, and then grabbed my toothbrush. My mom and Nana were dressed and gone, and there was a pair of jeans and a button-down top on my newly made bed.

My mom couldn't help herself sometimes. She'd worked to take care of her and Nana for years. My parents split up when I was in college, and my grandfather died shortly after Jean-Marc was born. She had resisted retiring when I moved in with them months ago, but I had insisted, saying it was my turn to take care of them.

Honestly, I hated seeing her work so hard at sixty-six. She and Nana had both earned time to have fun. When Hattie hired me, she paid me more than I had made at the hospital, which ultimately convinced my mom it was alright. Fate had to be driving events in my life. It was the best explanation I could come up with to lead me to where I was today.

How else would I be in the right place to help Harry and his aunt, or Lilith and her daughter? Not to mention the feral shifter and Selene. Speaking of the ghoul, I needed to get that damn demon out of her. I dried off and slipped into my clothes before I headed downstairs.

A smile spread across my face when I heard laughter in the kitchen. My tribe included so much more than I could ever have imagined. Layla, Mythia, Tsekani, and Evanora. Even Thicket had come to mean a lot to me.

Nina was teasing Tsekani about something while Nana told Mythia about finding Aidoneus in my bed this morning. Aidon sat next to her with a smile on his face and joy in his eyes. I grabbed a pastry from the platter and joined them.

"Aidon said you've got an idea about how to help Selene," Nina said when she saw me.

"Good morning to you, too, Nina. How did you sleep? Well, I hope." My sixteen-year-old daughter rolled her eyes, making me smile. "Sorry, sweetheart. Couldn't resist. Yes, I got the idea when I was unraveling the spell on Zack last night."

"It was the free-form spell work, wasn't it?" Tarja sauntered through the open backdoor and jumped onto the stool Aidoneus had vacated to stand next to me.

I grabbed a plate, began tearing off the pastry pieces, and put them on the saucer in front of her. "It was actually. I unraveled a Dark enchantment. Why can't I unravel a demon's hold?"

There were six pairs of eyes on me, and it was unnerving. Aidoneus set the pastry down he was about to bite and brushed off his hands. "It's never been done before, so I can't say if it's possible or not. But if there is anyone that can pull it off, you can. I say we give it a try."

"Let's do it close to the Hellmouth. It will be easier for you to banish the demon if we're next to the seal."

I tilted my head and looked at my familiar. "Can't you just send it home from anywhere like you did before?" It didn't make any sense that Tarja would recommend that we go to the Hellmouth.

"The Underworld is locked down, Queenie." Aidon ran his knuckles across my cheek. The simple touch made me feel sexier than getting all dolled up. "That means the only way in or out is through the Hellmouth. That's for everyone. And until Thanos gets his open, ours is the only one."

I had assumed the gods of the realm would be able to move freely. "So, the entrances you told me about around the world have now been closed? How do the dead get there?"

"The Hellmouth doesn't impair spirits that enter the realm. Otherwise, yes. The Underworld and its various entrances have been sealed off. We've moved one of the sentries to monitor the Hellmouth in the Underworld and will move others as soon as more are created."

That soured my stomach. He wanted my help to get the other Pleiades on board with the plan and open Hellmouths in their area. I didn't know the various witches at all, so I wouldn't be doing that.

Meeting the other Pleiades as soon as possible was on my growing to-do list. We had a lot to discuss, and if the Hellmouths came up, I would talk to them about it. Although, I understood why I felt so drained lately.

"Tsekani, would you drive Nana and my mom to the site? We will meet you over there with Selene."

Tseki extended a hand to Nana. "It would be my pleasure."

"Can I drive this time?" Nana asked as they headed for the six-bay garage.

I'd been in there once and couldn't believe the number of cars Hattie had. It made me uncomfortable to know I'd been given so much, so I relied on Layla and Tseki to pull the cars into the driveway when I went somewhere.

"Can you get Selene while I help Mythia clean up?"

Aidon bent and pressed a kiss to my lips, lingering longer than last time he'd kissed me. He was getting more and more open with his affections, about which I had mixed feelings.

"I'll be right back," Aidon promised.

"He's entering the mating dance with you," Mythia said as we watched him go down the stairs.

My gut instinct was to stick my head in the sand and not discuss this any further. I was a mundie and clueless about a lot. Still, I had read enough of the family grimoire to know that something bound two individuals by more than a piece of paper. It often went soul-deep.

"What exactly does that mean?"

"Precisely what you suspect." I glanced down at my familiar, used to her snooping by now. *"Aidoneus is in the dance without a partner right now. You haven't decided to choose him, as well, so he is taking the risk of letting himself fall down that path before*

you're ready. His faith in you astounds me. I've never seen such devotion or power. The magic you two do together is unparalleled."

I chewed on my bottom lip, and I considered Tarja's words. I was saved from responding by Aidoneus returning with Selene over his shoulder. "Ready to go?"

"Yep. Coming?" I asked my familiar.

I swear Tarja narrowed her eyes at me before she jumped down and walked outside. "Sorry I didn't end up helping you, Thia."

The tiny pixie flew to my side and kept pace with us as we traveled across the yard toward Aidoneus's house and the Hellmouth. "I never expected you to help. It's my job. You pay me too much to do it, so I feel guilty when your mom helps. I would hate it if you did too. I'm perfectly capable of cleaning the house and feeding the family."

I turned to the side and noticed the way her chin lifted into the air. "I meant no offense. I'm not used to anyone doing anything for me. For twenty years, I did everything in the house and for the kids and had no help. Granted, I didn't do a perfect job because I worked forty-eight hours a week, if not more. I could have used you when the kids were little."

"Maybe someday we will have little ones in the house that I can look after."

I chuckled at Mythia. I was forty-three-years-old-past childbearing years. "Isn't Nana enough work?"

"She keeps me on my toes, that's for sure."

"Who does?" Nana asked as we reached the site. She was sitting on the ATV Tsekani used to drive them over.

I was surprised to see the ground cover was coming back already. It was a relief because it was heartbreaking to see the destruction of so many plants. "You, Nana. The seal isn't driving you guys away like it did last night. I'm not sure if that's good or bad."

"You're casting a bubble around everyone present. That's the only reason they aren't running away."

"I had no idea. No wonder I'm drained all the time. Between the everyday chaos, the Hellmouth, and doing magic without knowing, I'm surprised I'm even functioning."

Aidoneus set Selene down on the ground a foot from the Hellmouth. "That's because you're an incredibly powerful queen. Are you ready to make history?"

"Not really. Stand back in case this goes wrong." Aidoneus rubbed my back then stood beside Nina and my mom. They were the most vulnerable if I messed this up.

I closed my eyes and erased all thoughts from my mind except removing the demon's claws from Selene's mind and body. I didn't bother with the circle. I wasn't dealing with witch magic. This was an evil entity hijacking Selene against her will, and I wasn't going to let that stand.

I opened my senses to Selene. The demon was a dark figure crouching inside her body. *"Liberatio."* I targeted my magic at every spot I felt the demon had a hold of her.

A groan slipped from Selene, and her body jerked, but the demon remained in place. Although, his grasp was loosening. *"Liberatio!"* I poured even more energy into my spell. Aidoneus's arm wound around me when I stumbled.

I was nearing the end of my rope when dark mist lifted from her prone body and tried to dart away from the area. Aidoneus let me go and threw his hand out. "I don't think so, asshole. You're not getting away from this one. My father is waiting for you on the other side." The mist stopped moving and morphed into a black creature with fangs that curved over its lower jaw and spikes along its spine.

Aidon clenched his jaw and used telekinesis to force the demon over to the seal. He held it over the center and chanted in that foreign language of his. A dark red light shot up from the metal and encompassed the demon before dragging it down through the rune. The metal glowed red for several seconds after the monster disappeared.

Aidoneus scooped me up into his arms while I was still processing what had happened. "You did it, Queenie. You have saved ghouls everywhere from a horrific fate. Wait until I tell my dad you found a way around a couple gods that he's hated for centuries."

I groaned as he crushed me to him. "Let's wait to see if she wakes up."

"Is it gone?" Selene's voice made Aidoneus smile right before he set me down.

I crouched next to her. "Are you alright?"

"I'm famished. Otherwise, I have never felt better. I thought I was done for when the demon overtook me."

"Let's get you some ribs before you start snacking on the rest of us. You can tell us what it was like to be driven by a demon," Nana called out.

I looked at Selene, who was grinning from ear to ear. She was up and moving a second later, seemingly no worse for the wear. I would keep a close eye on her, just if there are side effects of the possession. That's another task checked off my list. If only the thing would actually get shorter. Every time I turned around, new ones were added.

STELLA PULLED into a parking spot in front of an ice cream shop in Rockland. My bestie came as soon as she heard I'd saved Selene then told me we needed to continue searching for the witch responsible. Stella was enjoying her role as my right-hand woman in these adventures.

She believed wholeheartedly that it was our job to police the magical world and reveled in it. So, here we were back in the town north of Camden to look for clues. I had no idea what to search for.

"Let's grab an ice cream, then you can do your thing," Stella suggested.

I laughed as I held the door open for my friend. "What is my thing?"

Stella glanced around the busy ice cream shop as we entered. "You know, using your powers to locate the bad ones."

I laughed nervously. What was she thinking? I shouldn't have worried. No one paid any attention to us. "You do know the chance is high that she isn't here. Just because Selene didn't fare so well here doesn't mean her tormentor will live down the road. Life doesn't hand me the culprits so easily."

Stella shrugged her shoulders. "We have to start somewhere."

"Welcome to Scoops. What can I get you today?" A young girl around Nina's age asked. Stella ordered a scoop of rocky road before I ordered some cinnamon ice cream. Treat in hand, we exited the shop and headed down the main drag of stores.

I licked the creamy cone as we passed two women with children. I continued eating while I opened my magical sensors. Months ago, after I fought Myrna, I struggled to block out everything magical in my surroundings, so Tarja worked with me daily to put up blocks that would always be active.

I sighed in relief when I wasn't hit with five dozen different signals at once. It had been Aidoneus who helped me open up in the first place when we were roaming around Mount Battie searching for Lilith after she'd gone missing.

"I don't sense anything."

Stella swallowed a bite of her ice cream cone. "It's alright.

We've only just started. We will keep walking through the area."

I grabbed her arm and pulled her to a stop. "No, you don't understand. I feel nothing. Even in the middle of the woods, I picked up four or five magical signatures. In the middle of a bustling town like this, I should pick up more than that."

Stella threw her uneaten cone away and pushed toward an alley two stores to our left. "Can you sense me?"

My heart started racing, and my chest tightened. "Not at all. What's happening?" I clutched my chest when my lungs refused to expand. "I can't breathe."

Stella's hands fluttered over my torso before she grabbed her cell from her purse. "Calm down, if you can. Let's head back to the car. I think we need to go to the hospital."

I shook my head from side to side then started bobbing it up and down. "I...can't." I stumbled along the sidewalk and fell into the passenger seat the second she opened the door.

I tried to access my magic, but nothing responded, and my chest got even tighter. I heard Stella talking to someone but couldn't make out anything that was said. I was too busy reaching for my power.

My heart grew tiny fists that were banging against my rib cage to relieve the crushing vice enclosing my organs. My fire. It was part of me. I called it up, and a small purple flame dripped to the floor of her car.

The carpet went up in flames, and Stella screamed before composing herself and smothering the fire. Stella's hand ran over my back, and some of the tension eased. "Don't worry, Phoebe. I'm taking you to the hospital. Tarja says not to use your magic right now. If you're having a health crisis, you can hurt yourself or someone else."

"Mom..." I gasped out.

Stella pulled into traffic and flipped around to head south. "Your mom and Aidoneus will be meeting us at the hospital. Your mom will be carrying Tarja in one of her big purses. Nana will come out if you need to stay overnight."

My mind whirled, and my heart raced while sweat dripped down my back. I was losing my shit. I could barely get tiny sips of oxygen through my gulping attempts to breathe.

Distract yourself. With what? My mom's big purses? I never understood why most women gradually started buying bigger and bigger bags as they got older until I had kids. You needed the space to carry snacks, diapers, extra clothes, and more. That habit only got worse the older we got, too. Nana carted every kind of medicine she might ever need, plus candy and gum. And she had a suitcase for a purse.

I had no idea what was happening to me, but for the first time since Myrna almost killed me months ago, I was afraid I wasn't going to live to see tomorrow.

CHAPTER 18

$\mathcal{M}$y chest eased a fraction the second they put me on high-flow oxygen. It hadn't taken long for the ER doctor to admit me. The EKG had them squawking like chickens before taking my blood. If I had to guess, they were looking for signs of an infection.

Aside from my sky-high heart rate and labored breathing, I could cook an egg on my skin with how high my temp was. My body started doing a shimmy-shake, and the nurse cursed before letting go of the needle sticking out of my arm.

The tourniquet above my elbow turned the plastic shield connected to the needle into a blood spout. A woman's voice ordered the nurse to give me a dose of lorazepam. Had to be a doctor. I didn't think I was having a seizure but wasn't a good judge at the moment.

"Is she going to be alright?" I wanted to reassure my daughter, but I was too busy biting my tongue to formulate words. I was seriously ill. I hadn't felt this bad, ever. I was still alive, which was something but far from out of the woods.

"We are doing everything we can to help your mother.

Her blood tests show signs of an infection, but we can't locate the source." That was definitely the doctor that had ordered the medication. "She will be taken for an MRI soon. After that, we should know more."

"Queenie," Aidoneus's voice soothed me. Or it could have been the meds taking effect. I stopped shaking and tried to take a deep breath but ended up choking. I couldn't respond yet, but I did shift my gaze to his worried sapphire eyes.

"They think she has an infection that's making her sick," my mom told Aidoneus.

Aidon ran a hand through his hair. "Is it from the patch on her heart that was done not that long ago?"

My view of Aidon was cut off when a woman in a white lab coat over scrubs bent over me and lifted my hospital gown. "How are you feeling? The steroids have opened your lungs. Your stats are climbing, and if it continues, we won't need a ventilator."

"Better," I croaked, then tried to swallow past cottonmouth.

"I'm doctor Rosen. You've been pretty out of it, so you likely don't recall me." The physician smiled at me. She had a friendly, open vibe which was rare.

She lowered her head and scanned my chest. "You must heal very fast. The sternotomy is completely healed, leaving behind only a thin pink line. The skin is starting to discolor and has a slight green cast. It might be bruising that is still healing, but it could mean an infection around the patch. We need to make sure it isn't in your heart, or you will be looking at another surgery."

How could I have missed that? I was trained to monitor wounds and the healing process. Clearly, I was losing my touch. My mom appeared on my other side, along with my daughter. Nina grabbed my hand, and I wanted to reassure her but needed more information. If I was septic, I had a long road ahead of me.

"Blood cultures?"

The doctor nodded her head. "Now that the seizure has passed, we can collect blood and run them. I will be back with the results of the MRI and will hopefully have more answers for you all."

"Thank you." The doctor gave me a smile and patted my shoulder before turning away.

The young woman that had been taking my blood was back. "Let's try this again." She removed the needle and slid it into another vein, then filled the culture bottles. She was fast and efficient and gone in no time.

Aidoneus replaced the nurse and bent to kiss my fore-head. "What happened? Stella was surprisingly calm when you couldn't breathe or work your magic. It kept me from losing control of my power and causing a hurricane or something."

I turned my hand over and threaded my fingers with his. "I don't think it's magic. Everything aches, and I feel sick. It's been building. I assumed the drain was from the Hellmouth. Now it seems it was this infection building steam."

"You need to watch out, Tarja," Nana called out. I glanced over in time to see Tarja jump from my mom's big, purple purse. The thing hid my familiar without a hint she was in there.

"It's alright, Nana." My words ended in a coughing fit that sent my mom to get me some ice water.

Nina brushed my hair from my forehead. "I can hide her when they come to take mom. My jacket is bulky."

"I can hide her from mortals. I can't hide her from the magical world, but mundies are no problem," Aidoneus said.

Soft paws landed on the edge of my bed when Tarja jumped up to join me. She crawled up the mattress, careful of the tubes coming out of my arms. *"Your body is working over-time. I feel it fighting something. If the doctors are right, this is the worst one I've encountered. Many of my charges have battled illness, but nothing has been like this."*

The worry in her mental voice was unmistakable. I couldn't imagine how many losses like Hattie she had experienced. I knew she'd been in the Silva family for generations. "The doctors are going to figure this out," Aidoneus reassured everyone. "They have a plan and seem pretty sure they know what is happening."

"Aidon is right. There's no reason to worry until we have more answers. Your body has been put through more than any other Pleaides in history. Typically, they aren't targeted often, except by the top of the witching world. The abuse you've been through has to take a toll on your body."

A knock on the door made everyone jolt. Several pairs of eyeballs moved to the wooden panel. Nina glanced at Tarja then Aidoneus before she lunged for my familiar. I bet she assumed Aidon hadn't hidden her because she could still see my familiar.

I opened my mouth to say something, but Tarja was stuffed in her jacket, and she moved behind my mom before the panel cracked and a young man came inside pushing a wheelchair. Too late to say anything now.

"Hi, Ms. Duedonne. I'm here to take you for your MRI. Do you think you can sit in a wheelchair?"

I started to answer, but Aidoneus scooped me up into his arms. "I'll carry her."

The orderly's eyes resembled fried eggs as they flared. I patted Aidon's chest. "I can go in the wheelchair." When he shifted his gaze to me, I could see he didn't want me out of his sight. "You can push it."

Aidon held me tighter for a second before he set me into the chair. The orderly fumbled with the tube for my oxygen but finally got it transferred to the portable tank on the back of the chair. The bags of fluid were easier to move over.

"Follow me," the orderly mumbled before he hurried out the door.

I was hyper-aware of Aidoneus pushing me and was side-tracked, so I nearly missed Stella as she stepped off the elevator the orderly was standing next to. "Hey, Pheebs. Going for some testing?"

"Yeah. I'll be back." My words were choppy as I gasped for breath. The tank wasn't as effective as being connected to the wall unit.

She nodded, and we entered the elevator. Aidon positioned us in the corner behind the orderly and ran his thumb across the back of my neck. My body tried to respond, but it didn't get very far. Having a fever and erratic breathing would do that to you. It was challenging to keep from asking him to pick me up again.

All his touch made me want to do was curl up in his arms and go to sleep. I would be safe with him. My heart skipped a beat, my chest tightened, and I was once again tired. I leaned my head on Aidoneus's forearm and closed my eyes.

The chair bumped as we exited the elevator and resumed a smooth ride as he pushed me down the halls. Aidon's masculine scent surrounded me, drowning out some of the harsh antiseptics of the hospital. That used to be my perfume, given how often I spent in this environment. After meeting Aidoneus, I prefer being surrounded by him.

"Place her on the table. You'll have to wait outside while we run the MRI."

I groaned. I wanted to stay right where I was. I opened my eyes and got an eyeful of a chest covered in tight fabric. Aidoneus placed me on the table with my head on the pillow.

"She needs a blanket. She's cold." Aidoneus's voice was a

sharp demand. I appreciated it because I was cold, but they would have asked if he'd given them a second.

"Relax, Yahweh. I ran a hand over his abdomen because that was all I could reach. "I'm alright. They've got me."

Aidon bent and placed a kiss on my lips before he strode from the room. He hovered a foot from the open door. The orderly approached me with a folded blanket. "It's fresh from the warmer." He looked over his shoulder quickly then laid it across my body. "He's intense, isn't he?"

I smiled. "You have no idea. He means well."

He returned my smile. "Oh, I know he does. As you probably know, we don't get many that love their wives as much as he does."

I let that go with a head bob. "Are you running scans without contrast first? Or will it just be the images with it?" I wasn't sure how long Aidoneus would be patient. Warning him would be a good idea.

"It'll be both. They need detailed images of the structures to look for signs of infection. The nurse will come in after the first round and give you the injection."

"Aidoneus," I said in a hoarse voice. I couldn't speak all that loud. "This will take about forty-five minutes. Maybe longer."

Aidoneus pointed to the linoleum floor where he stood. "I'll be right here."

The orderly placed a pair of large headphones over my ears, then pushed a button, and I was stuffed into the tube. Thankfully, I wasn't claustrophobic. The door shut, and a man was on a speaker giving me instructions.

The banging and knocking of the machine gathering images was loud despite the headphones and music playing through them. It made me wish the orderly had given me some earplugs instead. They typically asked what a patient preferred. The poor guy was off his game, thanks to

Aidoneus. All I could do was smile. Miles had never been that protective of me. In fact, no one had.

I thought about the events of the last few weeks while inside the machine. I needed to make sure Thicket has enough silver for the charms for shifters. And ask Tarja to teach Nina how to cast a spell on them to help make them. I needed to call Fiona and tell her about Selene and how she was free and ask if she knew how to help the ghoul. I couldn't leave her like she was.

Before I knew it, the guy was in there giving me a shot, and it didn't seem all that much longer before the scan was done altogether. By the time Aidoneus was wheeling me back into my room, I had a list a mile long of what I had to do. At the top was calling Lilith and apologizing for missing the board meeting at Silva, Inc. scheduled for this afternoon.

The doctor was waiting for us when we arrived, along with a resident and a nurse. "I have good and bad news, Ms. Duedonne. We discovered what is causing the infection and can deal with it right away. The bad news is you will have to have surgery right away before the infection can spread."

I twisted and put my hand on Aidoneus's arm. "I take it you want to prep me now."

Doctor Rosen rocked on her heels as she clutched a tablet to her chest. "That would be ideal. The infection hasn't reached your heart yet, but your kidneys are starting to struggle. We'd like to avoid further complications."

"Is there something you left in her that is causing this complication?" Aidoneus's growl made me cringe. Especially when the doctor went pale.

"There is a foreign object lodged in one of her lungs. It isn't something from her first surgery. It seems to be an abscess, but I won't know for sure until I get it out of there. The sooner we get it out, the faster you will have answers."

When I nodded my agreement, it signaled my family.

179

Nina and my mom rushed to me and embraced me. Nana and Stella were there a second later. "We love you, sweetheart." My mom's voice cracked.

Nina kissed my cheek and let go of me. I was a lucky woman. My family had my back regardless of the situation. "I love you all, too. I'm going to be alright. I know this seems fast, but it's promising. They know what to fix and aren't wasting time."

It helped to have worked in a hospital. I knew their urgency meant I faced serious issues, but I also knew their rapid response would only help me. Aidoneus picked me up and turned with me. I'd heard the squeak of the wheels and knew there would be a gurney waiting to take me to the OR.

He didn't ask for permission as he followed them until we reached the operating room, where he kissed me deeply. I heard someone telling him he couldn't stay there before the door to the room was closed.

I knew the routine and scooted over to the operating table before removing my robe and grabbing the blanket to cover up. A nurse prepped my chest while the anesthesiologist asked me to count backward from one hundred. I got to ninety when my eyes slipped closed. I could swear I saw Aidoneus standing in the corner of the room before everything went black.

* * *

"SHE LOOKS BETTER ALREADY. Whatever you took out of her cured her." What was Nana talking about? The second the question entered my mind, my memory flooded back, and I cracked open my eyes.

My lids were heavy, and my throat burned, but I could breathe easily. The constriction on my chest was gone. And, my magic was there, roaring in the center of my body. It was usually a hum. Whatever had happened had agitated it and pissed it off.

"She's awake," Stella called out from the foot of the bed.

Doctor Rosen's face appeared over me with a broad smile. "Welcome back. The surgery went very well. There was a foreign object working its way through the left lobe of your lung. It left a path of damage in its wake that I treated with an antibiotic lavage. If I hadn't read your records, I would have suspected you were shot."

She held up a small specimen jar and rattled it in front of me. When I reached for it, I had to hide that I was coming out of the anesthesia far faster than I should. There was a black stone inside the jar that carried negative energy. It had to have been shoved in me during the attack at the store. So much happened so fast and I didn't track it all.

I handed it to my mom and turned to the doctor. We had to keep that in our possession. "How much of the lobe did you have to remove? Will I need breathing treatments?"

"We took small samples to ensure there was no infection, but you shouldn't have any problems as you heal. We have you on antibiotics and will continue for the next few days while you're here. We will send you home with some as well, but you should make a full recovery."

"Thank you, doctor."

"You're welcome. Get some rest. The nurse will be in to check on you and give you pain meds."

I nodded and rubbed my chest. It hurt from being sliced open, but the absence of exhaustion was most profound. I felt the Hellmouth and realized it hadn't been draining me. It was the stone.

The second the door closed, Aidoneus held out his hand to my mother. She placed the jar in his palm and rubbed her arms. "This holds a Dark spell. I can feel it."

Do you know what it is? I wasn't able to sense it inside Phoebe, and that disturbs me deeply. I need to know exactly what it is so I can counteract it if she is ever injured again."

I bet my familiar would be convinced something was being planted on me anytime I fought in the future. Not that I blamed her. I hadn't felt it. I might have suspected something sooner if I hadn't had the Hellmouth taking energy. I attributed my symptoms to that.

Aidoneus whispered a word, and blue sparks shot from his fingers into the jar. They danced over the small surface before sinking into it. He sucked in a breath, and his eyes did a rendition of breakfast foods.

Aidoneus snarled before he took a couple deep breaths. "It's a siphon designed to drain you slowly as it worked its way to your heart where it would detonate and explode the organ. Whoever did this planned on stealing your power than killing you in a way no magic could counteract in time."

"It has to be Zaleria. She's the one Myrna mentioned before I killed her."

Stella picked up the jar then dropped it like she'd been burned. "I hope there aren't more after you, Phoebe. That is one nasty spell."

"You need to send the magical world a message," Nana interjected as she glared at the object like she could destroy it. "One that leaves no doubt about your powers. That way, any Tainted witch will think twice before attacking you."

"I agree, Amelia. Violence is the language of our world. Contenders for her power need to know she isn't an easy target because she used to be a mundie."

I pushed the button to lift the head of my bed and lowered it slightly when fire exploded in my chest. "Killing Myrna wasn't enough?"

"There were no witnesses. You killed everyone. The rumors you were responsible never gained wings. We should arrange a gathering that tempts Tainted to take a shot at you. Of course, we will

HELLMOUTH & HOT FLASHES

have the advantage and ensure you have a chance to show your strength."

"That's a problem for another day. I'll add it to my to-do list. The first thing I am going to do after I heal is find the witch that created Selene. Can someone else get rid of that thing?"

Aidoneus pressed a kiss to my temple. "I'll destroy it as soon as I leave the hospital. In the meantime, can I get you anything?"

"Cinnamon ice cream. I never got to eat mine earlier." My mom and Stella laughed while Nina sat on the edge of my bed. As the conversation shifted to favorite flavors, I met Aidoneus's gaze and melted into the emotion I saw there. He was too complex to decipher it accurately, but I knew without a doubt that he cared a lot about me.

CHAPTER 19

I cringed away from the black stone in Aidoneus's hand. It was smaller than a pea but packed a hefty punch. Layla stepped in between him and me, "Why the hell do you still have that?" Layla wasn't afraid of the son of Hades. She was one of the most loyal creatures I'd ever met. She would walk into the Underworld for me.

Aidon's forehead furrowed, and one corner of his mouth turned up. "I would never harm Phoebe. She means more to me than you can comprehend. I was about to destroy it when I got a flash of Phoebe's power. It stole my breath just like she does every time she walks into a room."

Tarja jumped onto the island and started purring. Static electricity traveled over her fur and crackled in the air. No one said anything while she did whatever it is she was doing.

"You just saved her life, Aidoneus. For the second time this week, I failed my charge. I hadn't questioned my ability to guide and protect her until now. I thought for sure I learned my lesson." For the first time since meeting her, Tarja's head dropped, and her pose shouted her regret.

I reached out and stroked her back, getting shocked in the

process. "I will not tolerate anyone disparaging my familiar. You have saved me more times than I can count since I became a witch. My family, too. You need to explain what is going on, so I can rebuke your assertion that you failed me. I can't sense anything but the sticky feel of the spell."

Tarja's tail twitched as she paced back and forth along the counter in front of Nana and me. I'd been home since the night before. "*The stone is the perfect Trojan horse. It not only pulls your power to it, but it collects it, as well. I never stopped to look deeper once I realized that it was stealing your energy. I wanted it away from you.*

"*Now that the urgency of the situation isn't weighing us down, I can see things clearly. There would be no reason to suck your power unless there was a way to transfer it to another witch. That stone can be used by a witch to bolster their powers. If it had killed you, the witch would have retrieved the stone after your death. Upon your death, it would have given another the Pleiades power.*"

"Is that similar to how Hattie gave her magic to my mom to save her?" Nina stood to the side, chewing on her thumbnail. I wanted to protect her from the danger and uncertainty of the situation. I didn't because she needed to know the score. This could be her life someday.

Tarja shook her head back and forth without pausing. "*Not at all. Hattie used a ritual designed to pass her powers onto her chosen heir. Hattie researched the ceremony and spell to give it to another. That can only be done of free will. And, it transferred everything with it. The business, house, cars, bank accounts, you name it.*"

"That's why I'm not healing as fast as last time. The stone has some of my powers." Clio had come and done a session with me in the hospital. This time there was no miraculous healing of the incision. I still had the staples running down the middle of my chest.

Tarja put a paw on my hand. *"I'm sorry, Phoebe. I should not remain in my position if I cannot properly look out for you."*

I looked into Tarja's green eyes. "I will say this only once. I expect you to listen. You did nothing wrong. And, you didn't miss it. It was hidden by strong magic, meant to lead you off track. I felt how much energy you used just now to see through the layers to the heart of that stone. Frankly, I'm surprised Aidon noticed it before destroying the thing. I cannot and will not do this without you, so stop saying you aren't fit for the role. Got me?"

"I will endeavor to never let you down again," Tarja promised and lifted her head high.

Aidoneus set the jar close to the edge and wrapped an arm around my shoulder. "The only reason I was able to pick up on it is because I'm a god. No one else could have. I continuously scan energy signatures all around me and rarely realize that I'm doing it even when I don't need to. It's an automatic alarm system I developed when I was young. The question is, how do we get the power back into you."

I tilted my head to the side so I could see him. "Do we even need to?"

"Yes," Tarja interjected. *"The Pleiades were created by the gods, as you know. During the process, they gave their subjects a complex, layered maze as a magical core. It's hard to navigate and control and vital to their survival. You're right. That's the reason you aren't healing. You're missing a piece of your unique puzzle."*

"Well, how the hell do you give it back to her? You can't put that thing back inside her. It was killing her," Nana demanded with a slap of the counter.

Tarja looked from her to Aidoneus to me. *"I have no idea. This has never happened before."*

Aidon tensed beside me. "I have some ideas, but I don't want to try them until the Dark spell is unraveled from the stone."

I rubbed my chest, wanting to go lay down. I should have known my luck wasn't that good. "I can't do it. I'm not strong enough right now. My chest is being held together with glue and wire. Trying to use that much magic can't be good for me."

Stella lifted a hand from the other side of the island where she stood next to my mom, both listening quietly. "There is no way you are going to try and do any magic. I've got you on this one. I bet even Nina could help me."

Nina gasped and shot wild eyes at me. "Do you think that's possible?"

Tarja shifted her gaze to Nina. *"You cannot perform the spell at this stage, but you have enough power to offer Stella a boost while she unravels it. But, let's do this outside, just in case. Mythia will be angry if we destroy her kitchen."*

The tiny pixie laughed, the sound like tinkling bells. "I wouldn't be happy. Neither would you guys since you prefer hanging out in here all the time."

Stella snatched the jar holding the stone and headed for the backyard. Aidoneus lifted me into his arms and carried me out after everyone had filed outside. Tarja was right behind us. He sat in one of the chairs around the tile table and settled me in his lap.

I snuggled into his hold and watched. It was odd to be on this side of magic practice for once. Stella and Nina stood in the grass with Stella holding the stone in one palm and Nina holding her free hand.

"What would you say to take apart the darkness, Pheebs? I don't want to accidentally harm your magic."

"You don't have the power to damage Phoebe's magic. There is no one living being or god that can. Her power was created by the gods Titan and Pleione. No one knows what it will take to destroy a Pleiade's power because doing so will cause chaos and likely bring about the end of the world. No one, not even the gods, want that."

187

"On that note. Use the spell, *separabo tenebris*," I told Stella. I didn't want to think about losing my magic or the end of the world. Both topics made me sick to my stomach.

"Alright. I can do this." I'd never seen Stella so nervous. She'd always jumped right in with both feet. I'd never seen her building her courage like this.

"You've got this, Stel. I know you can do this. Hold a clear picture of what you want to happen, then cast your spell."

Stella sucked in a breath and squeezed Nina's hand. She closed her eyes, then opened them and zeroed in on the stone. "*Separabo tenebris.*"

I held my breath and waited for something to happen. I leaned forward, willing some sign she was successful. Aidoneus ran his hand up and down my back, trying to relax me when nothing more happened. I wasn't sure what I expected, but it seemed like something should happen.

Stella's jaw clenched, and sweat broke out across Nina's brow. Stella's lips moved a couple more times as she repeated the chant. After the third time, black sparks flew off the small stone striking Stella and Nina.

I gasped and got to my feet, but Aidon held me back. The two were still concentrating, and they'd lose it if I interrupted. Electricity filled the air around us, making my hair stand out.

After what seemed like forever, but was really only a few seconds, maybe a minute, black smoke drifted up from the stone, smelling like rotten eggs. Stella gagged, and Mythia waved her hand, creating a wind that carried the stench away from us.

She crossed to us, still holding Nina's hand. "It's gone." She had a broad smile and dark circles under her eyes. Nina did, as well. "I almost gave up. I couldn't have unraveled that without Nina. You're going to be a powerhouse."

"Like my mom," she said with pride.

Stella dropped the stone into Aidoneus's palm. I held my hand over it and breathed a sigh of relief. My magic hummed in the small rock. "Now what? I still don't want this inside me."

Aidoneus shook his head from side to side. "I am going to put it back where it belongs."

I turned around to face him fully. "Is this another power you have because you're a god?"

His smirk was sexy as hell and made me want to kiss him. I shoved the desire away. I wanted my magic back before we got lost in our passions. "Something like that. Hold onto me."

My hands were on his shoulders before I took my next breath, and I braced myself as he placed the hand holding the stone over my heart. His sapphire gaze locked with mine, and he chanted a word in what I was beginning to suspect was ancient Greek. Yeah, I was slow. In my defense, I didn't know languages all that well.

Heat built from his skin into the stone and into me. My eyes flew wide, and I cried out as it felt like a needle was drilling into my heart. My fingers tightened on his shoulders as the pain increased to the point that it caused black spots to dance in my vision.

Aidoneus pressed his lips to mine, giving me his breath and some of his strength. For a second, his heart beat beside mine in my chest. A second later, it was gone, and so was the pain. I broke the kiss to take in a lungful of oxygen.

"Are you alright?" My mom asked from my right side.

My heart slammed against my rib cage, but it no longer felt like it would literally burst from my chest. "Yeah. I'm good. Stronger already." Aidon caught me when my legs turned to jelly and refused to hold me any longer.

"We need a margarita to celebrate," Nana announced.

"I'll make some tea," I replied. My magic was back, but it

had a lot of work to do on healing me. Margaritas would slow that down.

"I'll drink yours for you, Pheebs," Stella said as she wound her arm through mine.

"You can have anything you want," I promised.

"If Zaleria is the one that did this to you, she's more powerful than Myrna by a long shot. We need to find her before she gets even more magic."

Aidoneus nodded his head as he walked next to Stella and me. "I have agents looking for a Dark witch. We can't detect Tainted witches, but I think she's fully Turned."

I sank onto the stool at the island and sighed. Stella stood next to me while Nana took the seat next to mine. "Are we sure Zaleria isn't responsible for Selene? Perhaps she made her to get a mole inside your house."

Selene, who had been a silent observer the entire time, stepped forward. "I will never willingly make a move against you, Phoebe. I will happily remain in this house and never complain, so I cannot be used against you, either."

The ghoul had been apologizing for being so aggressive when she was possessed. I doubted she would ever stop trying to prove she meant no harm. It was one reason I wanted to help her as badly as I did.

"I doubt it. We have to assume Zaleria has a menagerie of demons. If she had sent one to possess Selene, it would have attacked immediately, rather than taking off in the opposite direction. It was running from her because it sensed she had enough power to harm it," Stella observed. My friend amazed me at her insight and how fast she picked stuff up in this magical world.

Mythia carried a basket full of stuff from the pantry. I could see the top of a bottle and the blender. The pixie set her things on the counter to the right of the island and got to work.

"We need to find her and stop her," Nana said. "We can't let her get close to Phoebe again. I can guarantee it was her behind the store when you were attacked, Phoebe. That cannot happen again."

I placed my hand over hers on the counter. "I know, Nana. And we will. The witch was calm and confident, like I expect Zaleria is, but the attack itself was a brash move. She's playing the long game. Trying to wear me down."

My mom snorted. "She needs to talk to Miles. What she's doing is only going to make you dig your heels in harder."

I laughed at that. My mom wasn't wrong. I didn't like being walked all over or forced into a corner. It was why I fought the divorce and my situation for six months before finally moving back home to Camden. I made Miles's life difficult and cost him more money in attorney fees. It was small consolation.

"Speaking of Zaleria," my mom continued, changing the subject slightly. "Do you think she's behind those other objects of power that are missing? Maybe if we find them, we can cripple her power base."

She referred to the objects I'd found when hunting for a missing ghost and her sewing machine. Lilith had discovered that a french press, rose quartz necklace, silver thimble, antique vase, and stainless-steel tea kettle had all gone missing. I had her and Bridget gathering information on these. So far, they'd added an antique cigar box and pair of four-inch Louboutins.

I shrugged my shoulders. "It makes sense that she might be behind the thefts. Honestly, I prefer focusing on these tasks. It's something concrete we can do. Trying to locate Zaleria feels like chasing rainbows."

"Agreed. I hate not getting anywhere. How can I help?"

I smiled at my mom. I was so glad she and Nana had accepted the existence of magic without too much freaking out. I needed them with me. "Lilith and Bridget have been compiling a list of previous owners and the original creator when they can find it. Do you want to follow up with them and help in the search? Finding out who had them, where they were stolen from, and when is our best bet at finally locating them."

"I'd be more than happy to," my mom said.

I sagged against Aidoneus, allowing him to keep me upright as Mythia started the blender, and everyone tossed around ideas for how best to discover information about previous owners for the objects of power. I smiled and listened to the conversation, adding my two cents every now and then.

These were the moments that created memories worth cherishing. It wasn't only the big moments but the everyday, mundane ones that showed you how loved you really were.

CHAPTER 20

*J*climbed into Stella's sedan and waved to my family, all standing on the porch. "Thanks for getting me out of the house. Mom and Nina won't stop hovering over me."

Stella pressed the gas and took off down my driveway. "You can't blame them. You've been injured frequently since becoming a witch, but this time they witnessed you almost dying. They're scared. I get it because I was terrified. I've never been so frightened in my life, Pheebs. Cut them some slack."

The throbbing ache in my chest twinged like it did routinely. The incision finally healed the day before yesterday, but significant damage had to be healed inside.

"You're right, and I have accepted their hovering without saying a word. But I am happy to be out of the house. I'm not used to being the one in bed while someone takes care of me. So, who are we meeting?"

"An elf named Keenor. He works from home, building apps. He moved to the area recently and wants a home on a cliff to remind him of his home in Eidothea during better times."

I looked forward to meeting the elf. "Does he know Fiona and her coven killed the evil king? Speaking of, I'm a member of the Backside of Forty, as well as Mystic Circle. I'm going to get Fiona to let you in, too. They might be in England, but they're worth joining."

Stella bounced in her seat and swerved across the dividing line, making the car heading in the opposite direction honk at her. "Do they have a ceremony when you join? I've wanted an official ceremony ever since I became a witch."

I laughed. It seemed like there should have been an official welcome into the magical world. I'd add that to my list and make it a priority. She deserved something special, given how her life had been upended. The changes excited her. She was the first to offer to help and had been instrumental in saving me when we discovered some of my magic was in the Dark stone.

I forgot what I was going to say when I caught sight of a skinny guy standing on the sidewalk. He had on a Nirvana t-shirt that took me back to my twenties and skinny jeans. The way he looked and what he wore made one assume he was into cosplay and was wearing some of his pointed ears.

"I'm going to guess that's Keenor."

Stella chuckled. "He walked into my office dressed like that, and no one batted an eye. My new receptionist, Leanne, wanted to ask him out because he was cute and not afraid to rock his cos-play ears around town."

"I bet there are countless women that think the same thing," I observed as she parked by the curb. My eyes traveled from him to the house behind him. "He's interested in this one? The next stiff wind is liable to blow if right off the cliff out back."

Stella narrowed her eyes and pursed her lips. "Keep that to yourself. We don't need him thinking this is a bad choice. You have no idea how hard it is to find homes in the magical world. Most of them want to live close to cities but want land for privacy. And, Fae need to be surrounded by nature."

I held up my hands. "I won't say anything, but I will be shocked if he wants this place."

Stella rolled her eyes and got out of the car. "Hey, Keenor. How are you today?"

The elf turned and smiled at us as we approached. "Good. I hope this isn't another interested buyer because I love this place so far."

Stella gave me a smirk before looking back at Keenor. "Not at all. This is Phoebe Duedonne. She's the Pleiades in this section of the world and my best friend. She just came along for the ride."

"Nice to meet you. Let's get inside." Keenor was already stepping onto the front walkway. The guy actually liked the house.

I scanned the exterior again and cringed when I saw the peeling white paint, missing shingles, and sagging wrap around porch. It was a two-story Victorian missing most of the gingerbread accents and a few of the windows. I loved old Victorian homes and bet it was stunning when it was first built.

It could be once again but would take significant work on Keenor's part. At one point in my life, I imagined buying an old place like this and restoring it. Now, I couldn't imagine ever having the time.

A shout startled me. My head snapped in Stella's direction to see her running toward the elf who was lying on the sidewalk. "What happened?"

"I don't know. He was approaching the door and was suddenly knocked down the walkway."

I grabbed Stella's arm and stopped her. "Wait a minute. It was likely a ward. I can't think of anything else that would repel magical creatures."

Stella crouched in her black heels, her pink suit jacket pulled tight across her chest as she reached for Keenor. "I can feel magic. What do we do now? Oh! Are we in danger?" Her voice lowered to a whisper on that last part.

I dropped to the ground with her and felt the spell. The magic powering it didn't feel like it was malevolent like I'd encountered around Myrna's house. That didn't mean much, but I wondered if this was simply an abandoned house with a ward from the previous owner that was still active.

"I don't think there's a Tainted on the premises. The spell is relatively weak. I'd bet we can cross it with little effort." I grabbed Keenor's leg and pulled him next to us outside the ward.

He blinked his blue eyes and groaned. "Damn, that hurt. Is the house not for sale after all?"

"Let us do some investigating. It could be a leftover ward or a new one," I told the elf. "Can you do me a favor and call a friend, just in case we run into problems when we go in there?"

One of his eyebrows rose to his hairline as he pushed himself up. "Are you sure you should go in there? If it is dangerous, I can look at another property."

I smiled and placed my phone in his hand. "This is just a precaution. I promised my family I wouldn't go into potentially dangerous situations alone. I'm not because I have Stella, but just in case shit goes sideways, I want you to call Layla and tell her to get here ASAP." I opened my phone, called up Layla's contact, grabbed Stella's hand, and tugged her to her feet.

She was shaking next to me, so I twined my fingers through hers. Energy tingled in warning as we got close to the stairs. The ward was set as close to the house as you could get. I had no idea why someone wouldn't protect all of their property or if it meant anything.

I sucked in a breath and drowned out Keenor talking to Layla behind us. I looked over at Stella. "Should we do this?"

Stella rolled her eyes. "You're letting your introduction to magic warp your opinion. Not everything is dangerous. I seriously doubt there is anyone inside that is going to jump out and attack us."

I shrugged my shoulders, unsure if she was right about that or not. So far, I had to say she was wrong. Practically everywhere I went lately, I'd been attacked. Even the grocery store FFS!

I opened my senses to see if there was any Dark energy nearby. There was the faintest hint of death. Where the heck had that come from? It must be my mind running away from me.

I imagined a shield in front of us with a lance that pierced magic. "*Magicis lanceam.*"

We strolled through the ward without effort and right up the porch steps. *Only to die when the rotting wood gives out under your feet. I clenched my teeth while Stella punched a code into the grey box on the door and removed a key.*

I didn't get a chance to relax once we were inside the house because a fireball came flying at me. Shoving Stella to the side, I dove in the opposite direction. Stella looked over at me from the floor where she sprawled.

"Do you see anyone?' She mouthed to me, and I shook my head.

The shadows moved in the kitchen a second later. I pointed in that direction and ran in a crouch. I caught Stella shaking her head back and forth rapidly. The witch was moving away from us. I needed to stop whoever this was. She might be squatting here for innocent reasons.

I plastered myself against the wall outside the kitchen, which had me facing Stella. It was then that I saw the burning rag in the entrance. Perhaps this wasn't a witch after all. I cast a shield around my body and stepped into the kitchen.

I crouched and had my fists in front of me, ready to fight, but my big moment went unnoticed. I caught the flash of dark brown hair flying behind a woman as she fled out the backdoor.

I passed a door that led to what I assumed was a basement. The smell from down there was vile. I'd check it out later. For now, I ran outside and threw my hands out. I never voiced the spell when I wanted, but the woman stopped so suddenly, she landed on her ass.

"Oh my God, you did that without saying anything," Stella blurted.

Shocked, I turned and inclined my head. "I don't know how." I screeched and jumped when the dirt moved beneath my feet.

Bones pushed through the dirt where I had been standing. Stella raced to me, jumping over holes that popped up every foot or so. Something latched onto the back of my leg, digging sharp talons through my pants.

I lifted my leg and shook it, trying to dislodge the zombie cat that clung to me. It was mostly bones, with a few patches of rotting flesh and fur. My eyes narrowed. These creatures weren't kept away by my spell.

"You can't hurt my creatures, witch."

I spun around, almost having forgotten about the woman. "Who are you?'

She walked toward me, not running now when she had dozens of dead animals crawling out of the ground and attacking us. When she got close, she tilted her head and flared her nostrils.

"You have one of mine." The accusation was spat at me.

"What are you talking about? I don't even know who you are." I jumped when Stella touched my shoulder.

"Sorry. I think she's a necromancer."

"She gets it. Give me back, Selene," the necromancer demanded.

I took a step back, my hand to my chest, and tripped over a large dog that was all bones. Its entire body crumpled when I landed on it, but its head latched onto my arm. Blood dripped around the sharp teeth.

Stella kicked some other animals away from us. I tried to pry the head off me but couldn't with one hand. Stella jerked her head to the side, then crouched and pulled the two halves of the skull.

It took me a few minutes to realize she was trying to tell me. *"Ferrum."* I directed my punch to the woman's mid-section. She went sailing across the yard. Stella tossed the dog skull toward the cliff and continued stomping on boney bodies.

Keenor ran around the side of the house and stopped short. "I heard screaming. What the...I see you found the witch."

"She's a necro and using the dead to attack us. Help me knock her out. I want to confine her." It would be easier if he could use wind to keep her off balance. I didn't know too much about necros, but I knew they weren't inherently evil from what little I did. I wanted to get a read on this one. And ask why she brought Selene back.

The wind caught me, and I started rolling toward the cliff with Stella right beside me. "Keenor!" My scream was carried away by the wind. Stella grabbed me as we were pushed closer to the cliff.

Bodies passed by us, and I glanced around frantically for something to grab onto but found nothing. I needed to amplify my voice so I could get his attention. "Keenor!" The wind cut off abruptly, and I collapsed, banging my cheek on a skull.

The animals had stopped moving. I needed to cut the necro off from her magic. I jumped up and scanned the yard, not considering it wasn't a possible task. I turned in a circle. "Where is she?"

Keenor's face fell, and he walked to the edge of the cliff and pointed. Stella and I joined him. "Shit! That's awful," Stella exclaimed.

My shoulders dropped. The necro was splattered all over the rocks below. I wouldn't get answers out of her now. "Dammit, I wanted to talk to her."

"I'm sorry. I was freaked out when a squirrel flew at my face and lost it." Keenor shuffled his feet and kicked a tiny rib.

"It's alright. We're alive, and that's all that matters. On the bright side, there won't be any dead animals buried in your backyard if you buy the property." I smiled and brushed the dirt off my clothes, wincing when I saw the holes in my arm from the dog.

Stella patted him on the shoulder. "Are you ready to see this house? I think there will be some cleanup needed in the basement, but it has good bones."

"Is this a normal day for you guys? Is this normal for a woman your age?" Keenor looked from me to Stella with a grimace on his face.

We locked gazes and started laughing. I clutched my stomach. "Yes, Keenor. This seems to be an average day for us lately."

Layla and Tsekani came running around the side of the house and slowed when they saw we weren't in danger. "You have this under control?"

I nodded and started for the house. "We do. Keenor here

blew the necros off the cliff. Can you shift tonight, Tsekani, and clean her up before mundies catch sight of her. It will delay the sale of the house to Keenor and raise questions we can't answer."

"No problem. I might be able to climb down and do it now," he said as he approached the edge. Stella, Keenor, and I continued to the house. After we showed the house, I needed to call Fiona. I needed to ask about how to give Selene her soul back yet. It was priority number one on my to-do list. The rest could come after that.

Download the next book in the Mystical Midlife in Maine series, Holiday With Hades HERE! Then turn the page for a preview.

EXCERPT FROM HOLIDAYS WITH HADES BOOK #4

"*A*re you kidding me? I can't imagine Hattie being shy like that. She always spoke her mind without apology." I laughed as Tarja told us stories about a fifteen-year-old Hattie trying to tell the boy she liked that she wanted to date him.

I heard the scratchy coughing laugh of my familiar fill my head. *"Hattie was young and insecure once, despite being the heir to the Pleaides witch power. Back then, she was gangly and awkward. And completely in love with James. She thought the sun and moon hung in that warlock's brown eyes."*

Mythia hovered near the Christmas tree with a garland strand in her hand. She paused in winding it around the branches. "I remember when she invited James over to the house to study. She cast a spell to make her boobs bigger, and they ended up so big the buttons on her shirt popped open. Her mother was mortified that she flashed James. Of course, he didn't mind it at all."

My son laughed. "I bet he didn't. What happened? Did they date and eventually get married?" My heart ached at his question. He didn't know Hattie never married. And, he had no idea she was brutally attacked and rendered barren.

Tarja shook her head from side to side before she batted a glass ball toward the tree. *"Hattie never dated James and never married. She threw herself into creating a corporation that would be able to support magical kind. She had a dream of giving witches and warlocks a safe place to work where they didn't have to fear losing control of their magic."* I was distracted by what Tarja was saying. She used her familiar powers to make the glass decoration float before settling on one of the branches.

"I wish I had that kind of control over my magic," I blurted. My familiar's abilities always made me feel like an imposter. It didn't help that I wasn't born to cast spells and use magic. I was a mundane human until six months ago.

Nana snorted. "Tarja's had centuries to perfect her craft where you've only been at it for a few months. You shouldn't be so hard on yourself. You've accomplished far more than I expected this soon."

My mom inclined her head. "Nana is right, sweetie. Stop beating yourself up and expecting so much."

I sighed and unplugged the strand of white lights. My favorite part of the holidays was decorating the tree and enjoying the bulbs that twinkled in the branches. "I know what you both are saying is true, but I can't help but feel like there's something wrong with me. I mean, look at Stella. She doesn't have nearly as many issues as I do with my casting and potion-making. It comes so easy for her."

Tarja placed a paw on my leg and looked at me with solemn eyes. *"Ordinary witches aren't the best people to judge your performance against. They wield a fraction of the energy coursing through your body. While they're channeling the equivalent of a blow torch, you're funneling a volcano. That takes time and practice to master. Hattie blew up half of this house when she was learning. It had to be rebuilt after her first lessons."*

My eyes widened, and my chest warmed. I'd become far closer than I ever could have imagined to my familiar over the past six months. I hardly remembered how I used to think Tarja was a spoiled feline and Hattie a crazy cat lady. "I'll have to keep that in mind. I love this house and would hate to blow it up."

"I don't know. I could use a bigger closet," Nana said as she handed my mom the ornament with my handprint that I made in elementary school.

I snorted and shook my head. "You don't need anything else. You use my closet and Hattie's clothes more than you do your own."

Jean-Marc chuckled. "Your closet is bigger than three of my dorm rooms, Nana. Mom's right. You have plenty of room in there. By the way, mom. Is your boyfriend coming over to help decorate?"

My heart skipped several beats, and my body lit on fire at the mere mention of Aidoneus. "I wouldn't call him my boyfriend, Jean-Marc. And, I didn't invite him over."

One of my son's eyebrows lifts to his hairline. "Well, then what do you consider him? You're obviously in a relationship. There was no mistaking how much he liked you when I was here a couple months ago. And, I know you two have only gotten closer since I returned to school."

I scowled at my oldest child. I didn't want to think about this at the moment. Let alone defend it to him. Their father burned me too badly for me to trust easily. I wanted to take things slow with Aidon. "I'm not entirely sure what we are. We like each other, and he helps when things go sideways with the magical beings in town. We also watch over the Hellmouth together. Maybe it's that bond we share that makes you think we are so close."

Nina picked up the popcorn strand she just finished and draped one corner on the tree. "It's not the Hellmouth, mom.

And it isn't the demons or other crises that have made you two close. From the first day you met him, there has been some connection between the two of you."

Nana gestured with her hands. The crystal icicle she held glinted like a weapon from the strands hanging on the tree in the low lighting. "Nina is right, Pheeb. I never have believed in love at first sight or soul mates, but the way he looks at you had me rethinking my position on the topic. There's no way you can deny what the two of you share."

My cheeks heated as I stood behind the Douglas fir while gathering my composure. A secret part of me wanted to believe what they were saying to me. Losing Aidon like I did Miles wouldn't be something I got over easily.

My ex-husband, Miles, was a selfish prick and always had been. I was too infatuated to see him clearly when I was younger, though. As a twenty-something young woman in college, I thought he hung the stars and moon. When I finished my nursing program, he was in medical school, studying to be a cardiothoracic surgeon. Miles seemed like the perfect guy back then.

Now, I was dating an honest to goodness god that thought I was gorgeous, intelligent, and talented. And he is considerate in bed, giving me orgasm after orgasm. There was no question he was better than my ex.

Good thing you aren't that young, stupid woman anymore. You might let this god slip through your fingers while pursuing a man that couldn't be bothered to see to your pleasure for over a decade.

I attached the next strand of lights and stepped out from behind the tree. "I do not deny anything, Nana. But he is a god with thousands of years of experience. I'm hardly more than a mundie." I left out the part about how worried I was that I wouldn't be able to hold his interest for long.

My mother shrugged her shoulders. "You're making Nana's point for her, sweetheart. Aidon has had countless experiences and likely been with more women than I can fathom. And yet, he's completely besotted with you. He wouldn't be if you were just an ordinary woman. You're a rare gem, Phoebe. One he's lucky to know."

I choked out a laugh. Her words hit home. She was absolutely right about everything she said, but embracing that belief was dangerous. "Let's talk about something else. How has your magic been, Jean-Marc?"

My son shot me a look that said he was going to protest, but it quickly vanished. Likely because he could see how much I did not want to discuss this topic anymore. "It's been wonky. I can't predict when it's going to act up. I set my philosophy professor's textbook on fire a few weeks ago and met a witch in my class when I did. Emlyn's amazing, mom. She took me to the ley lines and taught me how to draw from the energy surrounding us. That helped stabilize me."

Nina's eyes went wide, and she smirked at her brother. Uh oh. "Oooo. You love her, don't you? Have you kissed her yet? I bet she spends more nights in your dorm room than in her own. Leave it to you to fall for the first witch you meet."

Jean-Marc smacked Nina's shoulder. "Shut up, turd. You're just jealous because you don't have any witch or warlock friends."

Nina thrust her hands onto her hips and growled at her brother. "I do too. Mom runs the coven in Camden, idiot. I have more witch and warlock friends than you can imagine. Plus, I'm friends with pixies, shifters, and vampires."

That got my attention. "Vampires? Since when have you made a vampire friend, young lady?"

Nina rolled her eyes and waved a hand through the air. "I met him at school, mom. Keir was born a vampire and doesn't feed on people. His parents get blood from the blood banks."

I nudged Tarja with my toes. "*Do I need to be worried a*

vampire attends school with Nina? Aren't they bloodthirsty demons?"

My familiar didn't look at me as she responded. *"There are vampires that refuse to follow decorum and use caution, but most take steps to keep their existence hidden. The dangerous clans are ruthless. I can't see them sending their kids to school. For the most part, they aren't blood-thirsty creatures. In fact, the majority are like any paranormal and would never hurt another in pursuit of blood. Don't judge Keir before you meet him."*

"I won't. Thank you." I shifted my focus to Jean-Marc. "So, Emlyn, huh? What's she like?" I didn't trust many witches outside my immediate circle after my experience with Myrna.

Jean-Marc's cheeks pinkened, and he averted his gaze and started looking through our box of ornaments. "She's super smart. And a great witch. She's a natural at casting balls of light. She doesn't even seem to think about it. She's funny, too. It's easy to hang with her. We have no awkward moments, and she seems to understand what I feel before I do, so she's got a lot of insight."

My little guy was definitely falling for this witch. It was evident in the way he lit up when he talked about her. I smiled and continued with the lights. "Emlyn sounds wonderful. I can't wait to meet her."

"Does she know mom's the new Pleiades?" Nina asked as she continued grabbing decorations from the boxes.

I walked over and put the Santas back. The magical world celebrated Yule and Winter Solstice, not Christmas. And I was determined to have a mix of traditions to form our own without offending my new friends or family.

"Let's leave the Santas out of the festivities this year. They don't fit Yule, and we are developing a new path for the holidays this year." Nina nodded her head, and I focused on the question she'd asked her brother. "Have you told her about me?"

Jean-Marc lowered his eyes and chewed his lower lip. "I haven't said anything to her. I didn't know what to say. You've had enough people attacking you, and while I think she's great, she might have a crazy mom or something. The last thing I want is to cause more problems for you, mom."

Tears sprang to my eyes, and I wrapped my son in a hug. "I'm not sure if that's necessary, but thank you for thinking of me." I released him. "What do you think, Tarja?"

My familiar stretched her back. *"Few witches pose a threat to you. Most will worship the ground you walk on. We will know if her family is Tainted when we meet her. Even if her parents have Turned, they will imprint her as their daughter that we can detect. Although, chances are good her parents work for you. Thousands of witches and warlocks do."*

Hearing about the company I inherited made me feel guilty. I'd been to the offices in Camden but haven't traveled to others yet, and I needed to. Lilith had been hounding me to make plans to meet the other site managers and see production at the various plants throughout the globe.

A knock at the door interrupted my response. "I'll get it." I'd bet it was Stella. Her husband worked tonight, and she was no doubt bored. Or afraid to be home with her kids. She'd told her family she was a witch, and they'd been stand-offish with her ever since.

My resident ghoul passed me carrying a tray of hot cocoas and a slab of ribs. I hope she didn't get barbeque sauce in the chocolate concoction like she did last time. Seeing her sparked my guilt over not having the answers for how to give her a soul. It was the only way to protect her from future possession. She hadn't left the house in longer than I cared to admit. Not that I blamed her.

She had no soul inhabiting her body as a ghoul, so it was

like chumming the ocean on a shark expedition. Unholy creatures flocked to her like flies to shit. The stories of zombies had to have originated from possessed ghouls. Beings from the Underworld loved death and destruction, and inside, a being like Selene could devour an entire town in a week.

A smile spread across my face the second I opened the door and laid eyes on the guy darkening my doorstep. "Aidon! What are you doing here? Please tell me there aren't demons we have to go hunt down. Selene just made hot cocoa, and we're decorating the house."

Aidoneus smirked and sauntered into the house as he reached for me. His hands landed on my hips, and his body heat obliterated the cold air seeping inside the open front door. I barely noticed when he kicked the panel closed because his mouth descended on mine and stole my ability to think straight.

My world narrowed down to god embracing me and how he was kissing me senseless. His lips were ravenous, and his hands roamed over my backside before squeezing. I was struck with the urge to rip our clothes off and take him right then and there.

The sound of a throat clearing brought me back to Earth with a crash. The sound was more profound than anyone living in the house, which told me it was my son. I broke away from Aidon's mouth with my face heating with embarrassment at being caught.

Jean-Marc had a knowing smirk on his face. "Are you certain he's not your boyfriend, mom? I don't go around kissing friends or acquaintances."

I rolled my eyes and headed into the living room. "I'm not sure what Aidon and I are. We have no need to put a label on it. I think we're both beyond needing anything so trivial."

Aidoneus caught up with me and wrapped an arm around

my waist, tugging me closer to him as I walked. The action nearly made me fall into him before I caught my balance. "My father would disagree with you, Queenie. He's coming here to meet the witch that stole my heart and claims to be my mate."

I stop, making him bump into my shoulder as I whirl around and face him. "What did you just say?"

"He said his dad is coming to meet you, Phoebe. You might want to get a CT scan before he arrives to ensure you aren't suffering from brain damage. You did take several hits to the skull a couple months ago," Nana shared, trying to be helpful.

Aidoneus cupped my cheek. "He's upset I'm not in his realm anymore, and my mother insisted on seeing me for the holidays. So he decided he'd use the trip as an opportunity to meet the woman that captured my heart."

My heart was racing so fast I thought I was going to pass out. I had to bend over and brace myself on my knees. My breath got caught in my throat. A fine sheen of sweat covered my entire body a second later as my hormones dropped from the high of a few minutes ago.

A hand-rubbed up and down my back. I turned my head to look up at Aidon. He gave me a reassuring smile. Too bad it did nothing to abate my terror. "There's no reason to panic, Pheebs. He's going to love you. Well, I know my mom will like you for sure. Dad is another story altogether. He thinks I'm making the same mistakes he did when he mated my mother. He hates being away from her half of the year, but that was the only deal her mother was willing to make at the time."

Jean-Marc stepped forward. "Is he going to try and make my mom live in the Underworld half the time? She can't leave Earth."

I stood up straight and grabbed my son's hand. "I'm not

going anywhere as exotic as another realm, peanut. And, I don't think meeting your dad is a good idea. I'm a middle-aged woman with an attitude and a sarcastic mouth. He already blames me for you living here. We don't need to add rocket fuel to the fire."

My mother put her hands on her hips, twinkle lights dangling from one hand. "Phoebe Alicia Duedonne. You will not talk negatively about yourself. I made you from scratch and did a damn good job if I do say so myself. You're beautiful, intelligent, caring, and as loyal as they come. Hades would be lucky if you decided to mate his son. And I'll tell him that when I meet him."

Tears sprang to my eyes, and I had to choke back the emotion burning in my throat. I was on a freaking roller coaster with no restraints and swore I was going to fly off any second. "I don't think you need to tell the God Hades anything, mom. I like you in one piece. But I needed that reminder. I am who I am, and I won't apologize for that. It took me months to start loving myself after Miles, and I'm not going to let anyone, even a god make me feel bad about what I look like or who I am. That being said, are you sure meeting him is a good idea?"

"My dad's bark is worse than his bite. He won't do anything knowing how much you mean to me. I'm more worried about him scaring you into bailing on us before we reach our full potential," Aidoneus admitted.

Nina set her cocoa down and looked from Aidon to me. "He can't break you guys up. The two of you are already tied together for eternity or something like that because of the Hellmouth, right? I'd be more worried he wants grandkids if I were you, mom." I gaped at my daughter. I never considered that.

"This is what's called dating, mom. Just so you're aware. Also, meeting the parents is a serious step," Jean-Marc added.

211

"Shut up, you two. You know if Aidon and I do get mated, then Hades is your step-grandfather." I laughed when Nina paled, and Jean-Marc vacillated between shaking and smiling. My son couldn't decide if that was cool or terrifying. I'd go with the latter if I were him.

Aidon laughed with me and shook his head. "No one needs to be afraid. My father is going to love everyone."

Famous last words, I thought. "When is he coming?"

"Winter Solstice," Aidon replied.

My heart dropped like a stone. "That's only a few days away. Oh my God. This house isn't ready for a god." I would have preferred to have the floors redone and get new furniture.

I never bothered to redo things after Hattie died. Her taste was old-fashioned for me, but doing anything different was a waste of money. Now I had to see what I could get accomplished before his arrival. The holidays were suddenly more stressful than when I was married to Miles. He insisted on perfection for his mother and father.

AUTHORS' NOTE

Review are like hugs. Sometimes awkward. Always welcome! It would mean the world to me if you can take five minutes and let others know how much you enjoyed my work.

Don't forget to visit my website: www.brendatrim.com and sign up for my newsletter, which is jam-packed with exciting news and monthly giveaways. Also, be sure to visit and like my Facebook page https://www.facebook.com/AuthorBrendaTrim to see my daily posts.

Never allow waiting to become a habit. Live your dreams and take risks. Life is happening now.

DREAM BIG!

XOXO,

Brenda

ALSO BY BRENDA TRIM

The Dark Warrior Alliance

Dream Warrior (Dark Warrior Alliance, Book 1)

Mystik Warrior (Dark Warrior Alliance, Book 2)

Pema's Storm (Dark Warrior Alliance, Book 3)

Isis' Betrayal (Dark Warrior Alliance, Book 4)

Deviant Warrior (Dark Warrior Alliance, Book 5)

Suvi's Revenge (Dark Warrior Alliance, Book 6)

Mistletoe & Mayhem (Dark Warrior Alliance, Novella)

Scarred Warrior (Dark Warrior Alliance, Book 7)

Heat in the Bayou (Dark Warrior Alliance, Novella, Book 7.5)

Hellbound Warrior (Dark Warrior Alliance, Book 8)

Isobel (Dark Warrior Alliance, Book 9)

Rogue Warrior (Dark Warrior Alliance, Book 10)

Shattered Warrior (Dark Warrior Alliance, Book 11)

King of Khoth (Dark Warrior Alliance, Book 12)

Ice Warrior (Dark Warrior Alliance, Book 13)

Fire Warrior (Dark Warrior Alliance, Book 14)

Ramiel (Dark Warrior Alliance, Book 15)

Rivaled Warrior (Dark Warrior Alliance, Book 16)

Dragon Knight of Khoth (Dark Warrior Alliance, Book 17)

Ayil (Dark Warrior Alliance, Book 18)

Guild Master (Dark Alliance Book 19)

Maven Warrior (Dark Alliance Book 20)

Sentinel of Khoth (Dark Alliance Book 21)

Araton (Dark Warrior Alliance Book 22)

Cambion Lord (Dark Warrior Alliance Book 23)

Omega (Dark Warrior Alliance Book 24)

Dark Warrior Alliance Boxsets:

Dark Warrior Alliance Boxset Books 1-4

Dark Warrior Alliance Boxset Books 5-8

Dark Warrior Alliance Boxset Books 9-12

Dark Warrior Alliance Boxset Books 13-16

Dark Warrior Alliance Boxset Books 17-20

Hollow Rock Shifters:

Captivity, Hollow Rock Shifters Book 1

Safe Haven, Hollow Rock Shifters Book 2

Alpha, Hollow Rock Shifters Book 3

Ravin, Hollow Rock Shifters Book 4

Impeached, Hollow Rock Shifters Book 5

Anarchy, Hollow Rock Shifters Book 6

Midlife Witchery:

Magical New Beginnings Book 1

Mind Over Magical Matters

Magical Twist

My Magical Life to Live

Forged in Magical Fire

Like a Fine Magical Wine

Mystical Midlife in Maine

Magical Makeover

Laugh Lines & Lost Things

Hellmouths & Hot Flashes

Bramble's Edge Academy:

Unearthing the Fae King

Masking the Fae King

Revealing the Fae King

Midnight Doms:

Her Vampire Bad Boy

Her Vampire Suspect

All Souls Night